THE SIXTH SENSE

SECRETS FROM BEYOND

HANGMAN

3

THE SIXTH SENSE

SECRETS FROM BEYOND

HANGMAN

3

By David Benjamin

SCHOLASTIC INC.
New York   Toronto   London   Auckland   Sydney
Mexico City   New Delhi   Hong Kong

ISBN 0-439-20272-8

12 11 10 9 8 7 6 5 4 3   1 2 3 4 5 6/0

Printed in the U.S.A.

First Scholastic printing, May 2001

For David Leventhal
(who can write much better than I can dance)
From David Levithan

THE SIXTH SENSE

SECRETS FROM BEYOND

HANGMAN

3

ONE

Cole Sear's school wasn't like other schools. It was originally built as a courthouse, prison, and gallows for the city of Philadelphia in the years following the American Revolution. For over a hundred years, people were tried, convicted, and killed within the building's walls. Many of them were guilty. Some of them proclaimed innocence with their dying breath.

When the building was turned into a private school, its deadly history was supposed to have come to an end. The blood-soaked cell floors were replaced with tidy panels of wood. The hangman's noose was packed away. The largest courtroom was dismantled and turned into a gymnasium. Students were never told about the building's gruesome past. But they found out anyway.

For most students, the school was the site for horrifying ghost stories and terrifying rumors. For Cole Sear, it was much more.

For Cole Sear, the horror was real.

Cole Sear could see dead people. He didn't ask to see dead people. Most of the time, he didn't *want* to see dead people. But he had no choice. They just appeared. And usually they wanted something from him.

Cole was haunted by his school's past. There were reminders everywhere: a family of runaway slaves who'd killed their violent master still hung from the rafters of a hallway; a deranged man sat curled up and weeping in the gymnasium, still hearing the guilty verdict pronounced by a judge who had died long ago; a boy Cole's age who'd been imprisoned and sentenced to a severe beating for stealing a horse could be heard calling out at noon each day.

Not all of the dead people were from so long ago. The ghost of a dead teacher had roamed the halls for years; she had died of a heart attack in the middle of class, without getting a chance to tell her husband about a secret bank account she'd been keeping.

Sometimes Cole could help. Sometimes he couldn't. He managed to get word to the dead teacher's husband about the secret account. But he couldn't help the family that hung from the rafters, or the man who wept at his dead-end future. They were beyond saving. They would haunt the school forever.

Cole knew he had to be strong, even though he was only eleven years old. He had to try to live a normal life. Sometimes the dead people left him alone. Sometimes he could get through an hour or two without thinking about them. He could laugh with his friends. He could get bored by his homework. He could round a corner without worrying about what was on the other side.

A couple of months had passed since his last experience with dead people, when he had helped try to find his best friend Jason's runaway brother. Since then, things had been fairly quiet.

Cole was able to focus on the lives of the undead, for a change. He was able to concentrate more in class, and his grades were improving. He was really excited about a history project he'd been assigned — his class was going to act out part of the Constitutional Convention, and each student was assigned a person to play. Cole, who used to go for whole weeks in class without saying a word, got the part of Ben Franklin — an important role.

Cole's class was taken to the school library to do research. The library was a new addition to the school, only a year or two old, but made to look like it had always been there. Nobody had been hanged in this library, or imprisoned.

Cole felt safe there.

There was a mad rush to the history section as soon as the class hit the library; Cole held back, as he usually did. He didn't like to be part of a crowd. When enough kids had come back to the library desks, Cole entered the twisted maze of bookshelves to find the remaining books about Benjamin Franklin. As he walked past the familiar rows, he could hear the whispers and giggles coming from other aisles — kids in his class using this time to gossip or play around, safely out of view from their teacher. Cole didn't listen in — he wasn't an eavesdropper. He knew they weren't talking about him, which was a change from the way things used to be.

As Cole approached the American history section, the lights dimmed. This happened from time to time in the library — in the rush to complete the new addition, some of the wiring was faulty. The heat didn't work too well either. Cole started to feel cold. Very cold . . .

But it wasn't the wiring — or the heat. It was something much, much worse.

All at once, he knew what was going to happen.

He could close his eyes. He could turn around. But it wouldn't matter.

The dead person would still appear.

It's happening again.

Cole knew it was better to face the problem head-on. So he didn't close his eyes. He didn't turn around.

As the lights dimmed further, a man came into view. A man Cole had never seen before.

A man with a noose around his neck.

Even though the library was carpeted, the man's footsteps thudded as if they were trudging across a hard floor. His clothes were old and worn, a dusty and dirty variation of the clothes Cole had seen in pictures of the Constitutional Convention. His skin was ice-pale, his eyes wide and dead. The rope clung tight around his neck, digging into the flesh. The noose was no longer attached to the gallows, but the dead man didn't seem to notice. He just walked forward, lost in the moment before hanging.

A chill spread through Cole's body — a wave that felt like death itself. Cole shivered and stepped back.

The dead man didn't say a word.

Instead he kept walking forward, heavy step after heavy step.

Then he lunged.

5

Cole was caught unprepared by the dead man's sudden movement. He fell back, reaching out to a bookshelf to break his fall. His hand landed on the spine of a book, toppling it to the floor. Cole slipped, hitting his head. The dead man took advantage and loomed over him.

Cole gulped for air. The dead man didn't breathe at all. Up close, Cole could see the burst blood vessels under his skin, the blood swimming in his eyes.

"What do you want?" Cole asked haltingly.

The man didn't answer. He just stared at Cole. Cole fought his instinct to turn away.

He couldn't let the dead man see he was scared. He had to pretend he was in control. *Even though I'm not.*

Cole could hear other voices now, coming closer.

The dead man nodded once and pointed somewhere behind Cole. Then he straightened up.

Cole didn't move. He would stay still until the dead man left.

A guttural sound escaped the dead man's mouth — something between a noise and a word. Cole couldn't understand. He wasn't sure he wanted to.

The lights dimmed again, then shot to their full brightness.

The dead man was gone.

A group of students turned into the aisle and saw Cole on the floor. Nobody said anything, but Cole could see them taking it all in. He reached behind his back for the book he'd knocked over, trying to pretend that he'd been sitting on the floor, reading it. Very casual. Nothing out of the ordinary.

The book lay open on the floor. When Cole looked at it, he nearly had a heart attack.

There, looking up at him, was the face of the dead man.

TWO

John Heginbotham.

Shaken, Cole brought the book back to a desk in the library and studied the picture. The noose and the blood-drenched eyes were gone. The clothes were clean, the pose dignified. And yet . . . it had to be the same man. John Heginbotham.

Cole turned back the page and started to read. There wasn't a lot about John Heginbotham, but it was a start.

The book was about the War of 1812, written by someone named David Rohlfing. Cole knew that the War of 1812 was fought between America and Great Britain, and that the threat had been so real that the British had invaded Washington D.C. before being turned back and defeated. But Cole had never heard of John Heginbotham before. Soon he found out why.

The book said that John Heginbotham had been a good friend of President Madison's, and had been a very important person in American political circles. Then, after the War of 1812 broke out, it was discovered that he had been passing secrets to the British. He was arrested and convicted of treason, one of the worst crimes in the new Constitution. Even though he protested his innocence, he was hanged on December 17, 1814, in Philadelphia.

That was all the book said. But Cole could imagine more.

If John Heginbotham was hanged in Philadelphia, he was almost definitely hanged in this very building, long before it had become a school. He was probably imprisoned here, too — kept in confinement until the moment came for him to be taken to the gallows. He was given his last meal, and then walked through the halls, his footsteps echoing off the floor. He yelled that he was innocent. Nobody believed him. He was taken to the room where he'd die. He was led up to the gallows and asked for his final words. The rope was put around his neck. A prayer was said. The trapdoor was opened and John Heginbotham's body fell. His neck snapped. He was dead.

And yet, he lived on.

Cole didn't know what he was supposed to do. Usually with the dead people there was something they wanted you to do for them — there was something to find, or someone to contact. But with Heginbotham it was different. Almost two hundred years had passed since he'd died. His world didn't exist anymore. Everyone he'd known was now dead. Only their great-great-great-great-grandchildren remained.

How could Cole possibly help?

The dead man's bloody stare came back to Cole, making him shiver.

Clearly, he wanted something . . . but what?

Cole turned back to the portrait. John Heginbotham looked like every other man from that point in history, with dull white hair and an equally dull expression. He looked like a leader, someone who would go far, someone who would be talked about in history classes as a Founding Father.

What had gone wrong?

The book didn't say. Cole would have to get his explanation elsewhere.

He would have to find out a way to figure out the mystery of John Heginbotham . . . because if he didn't, awful things were bound to occur.

Cole had learned the hard way: once dead people have found you, they don't like to be ignored. In fact, they will *make sure* they won't be ignored. They will do anything to keep your attention . . . even if it can bring you harm.

When the class period was over, Cole threw the War of 1812 book into his backpack and headed out of the library. As he crossed through the library's doorway, the book detector went off, sirens howling through the room, circular lights flashing above the desk.

Cole froze. What had he done? Then he remembered he'd forgotten to check out the book he'd taken. He spun around to return the book and his backpack fell open, spilling its contents to the floor. Cole had to block the library's only exit as he gathered his books and papers up. He could sense people staring at him. He heard someone snort with laughter.

Sheepishly, he headed back to the front desk. Luckily, the head librarian, Ms. Larkin, had a sense of humor about the whole thing.

"Don't worry about it," she said to Cole in a reassuring voice. "It happens all the time. I set the thing off at least two times a day myself and it screams bloody murder."

Cole signed out the book and thanked her. He was feeling a little less embarrassed . . . until he turned around and saw a few older kids staring at him.

"Hey, spaz — are the police coming to get you?" one said.

"Thanks for making us deaf, man," another chimed.

Ms. Larkin was out of earshot. The rest of Cole's class had already left. He was alone . . . and he felt alone.

A burly eighth-grader pushed to the front of the taunting crowd. Cole had seen him before, and knew he meant trouble. He always tried to avoid him . . . but this time, there was no getting around it.

"What are you looking at?" the kid said, coming closer.

"Look at him — I think he's going to wet his pants!" another kid yelled. The rest of the crowd laughed.

Cole didn't know what to do. If he said something, he'd only be inviting them to say something back. But if he kept his mouth shut, they'd think he was weak. They'd think they could pick on him at any time.

He decided to walk for the door.

"Hey," the burly kid said, stepping in his way. "Where do you think you're going?"

"I gotta go," Cole said quietly.

"When you gotta go, you gotta go!" the joker in the group yelled out, cracking everybody up again. Everybody except the bully standing in Cole's way.

"I'm not through with you," he said, staring Cole down, his expression dead serious.

"I really have to go," Cole said again, not trying to match the stare. He just wanted to leave. He could deal with the rest later.

The bully didn't look like he was going to move. Then Cole's friend Jason came into the library.

At first, Jason didn't seem to realize what was going on.

"Why are you still here?" he asked Cole. "I've been waiting for you outside."

Then it registered. He looked out of the corner of his eye and saw the kids looking at Cole, waiting for the next move.

Jason didn't miss a beat.

"C'mon," he said, ignoring everybody else. He led Cole right past the burly eighth-grader.

"You better watch out for Dennis, because Dennis is now on your case!" the bully yelled out, clearly referring to himself.

Cole didn't look back. When he got outside the library, away from everyone else, he felt the tension leave his body. If he'd really thought about it, he would have been scared back there. But he'd learned to not think about it. He'd learned how to keep the fear hidden, until it grew too strong to be controlled.

"What was that about?" Jason asked.

"I don't know," Cole said. "I set off the book alarm. They took it personally."

"Jerks." Jason sighed.

Ahead, in the hallway, Cole could see John Heginbotham with the noose around his neck. The other students walked around him, unaware.

Cole stopped.

"Cole?" Jason asked. "What's up?"

Cole couldn't tell him. Even if he thought for a second that Jason could believe him, he just couldn't tell him. There were only two people in the world who knew that Cole could see dead people — his mom and a detective in the Philadelphia Police Department named James Brown. That was enough for Cole. He didn't want his secret to get out. Because if it did, it would ruin his life.

"Is something wrong?" Jason kept up his questions. "Is it those guys back there?"

Cole shook his head. "It's nothing."

Jason looked at him hard for a second, then shrugged. He knew Cole was lying — Cole could tell. But he wasn't going to force it.

Cole wondered how long he could get away with it. How long would it be before Jason got sick of him and his secrets?

Best friends are supposed to know everything about each other. But there were some things about Cole that Jason would never, ever know.

Cole could see John Heginbotham *so clearly*. He could hear the footsteps, mark the seconds between them. But Jason couldn't see him at all. Nobody else could. Cole wished for the moment that they could. He had fantasies of Jason saying to him, "Hey, who's that dead guy coming toward us?" Because then Cole wouldn't have to do it all by himself. Then he wouldn't be the only one the dead people haunted.

When Heginbotham saw Cole this time, he held back. He was keeping his distance, giving Cole some room.

He knew he had gotten through.

Very soon, he would want results.

THREE

The dead man followed Cole to English class. He stood there, blocking the blackboard with his chalk-white skin. He stared at Cole without saying a word.

Cole tried to ignore him. But it was hard. Cole found that he couldn't look away. He was afraid of what the dead man might do. Heginbotham didn't look sad, like some dead people did. He looked angry and restless.

Cole thought he could hide his distraction. But twice when Ms. Grant called on him, he didn't have an answer for her. He couldn't see what was written on the board. After class was over, Ms. Grant asked him to stay back for a second.

Uh-oh, Cole thought. He remembered before, when the teachers had asked to see him after class.

It was never good news. They asked him why he was so out of it. They asked him if he was having trouble at home. They suggested he see the guidance counselor. They took him to task for late homework, or ignoring the lessons. They had no idea what was going on with him, but they thought that they did.

Ms. Grant was different, and Cole tried extra hard to do well in her class. She was new to the school and didn't know about his history. She saw him as a kid with promise, not as a kid with problems. Cole really wanted to prove her right.

But now she looked concerned.

"I lost you today, didn't I?" she asked, motioning Cole to come over to her desk. He turned his back to the dead man and walked over, thinking, *Please go away. Please leave me alone right now.*

"I'm sorry," Cole said to his teacher. "I guess I'm just tired."

Ms. Grant nodded. "Well, try to get some sleep, okay? I'm really proud of all the work you've been doing. Your report on *Tangerine* was excellent. You have a gift, Cole. You have to make sure you use it."

A gift . . . how many times had he been told by his mom or Detective Brown that his sixth sense was a gift? It hardly ever *felt* like a gift. Only when he helped someone. The rest of the time, it was the opposite of a gift. A gift was something you could give back, or return, or exchange. But the sense he had wasn't like that at all. There was no way of getting rid of it.

And now Ms. Grant was telling him he had another gift. Was it possible to have more than one?

"Try to stay awake for your next class," Ms. Grant said.

"I will," Cole assured her.

Then he left the classroom . . . with a dead man following at his heels, footsteps echoing through the halls.

Heginbotham trailed Cole for the rest of the school day. He stood at the front of each class, staring intently. He did not try to remove the noose from his neck. He did not try to speak. Instead he focused on Cole.

Cole didn't know what to do. Usually, the dead people left him alone at times. Usually, he had room to think. Heginbotham was different. *I have nothing else to do,* he seemed to say. *I am going to watch you until you get me what I want.*

Cole wasn't sure he could take it.

After school he went back to the library to find out more information about the dead man following him. But Ms. Larkin was out and the assistant librarian was swamped. Cole looked for more books about the War of 1812, but he seemed to have the only one available.

"You might want to check the city library," the assistant librarian suggested before going to deal with a kid who'd decided to eat some microfilm.

The Philadelphia Public Library wasn't that far away. Cole had been there a few times on class trips, or with his mother. Still, the thought of going there made him nervous.

The Philadelphia Public Library was full of dead people.

Cole didn't know why they gathered there. He couldn't even count how many there were. But there were definitely more than Cole could understand.

Still, if it was the only place to get information about John Heginbotham, Cole would have to go.

He heard the dead man's footsteps behind him as he walked to his locker, and then to the school door. But when he went through the door, the footsteps stopped. Cole turned and saw the dead man standing frozen behind him. The part of the noose that had dangled behind Heginbotham was now taut and raised. It would not let him go. He could not leave the building.

For the first time, his expression turned from fierce to imploring. *You must help me.*

Cole stared at him for a moment and gulped down his own fear. He didn't know if the dead man was tricking him now, or whether there really was a new truth to discover. Was he saying he was innocent — or was there some other unfinished business?

It was up to Cole to find out.

Cole walked into the main hallway of the Philadelphia Public Library and was immediately confronted by dead people. A man sat in front of his own statue, looking up, confused. Cole walked past and saw other people running their hands over the library's list of founders, their clothing style as old as the names engraved in the marble.

He usually went to the children's room, but this time he knew he'd have to scour through the adult books. He found a few books about the War of 1812 in the library's catalog computer, but none specifically about John Heginbotham. He also did an Internet search, but didn't find much.

The bookshelf aisles were scattered with dead people, most of them authors guarding the only copies of their books left in existence. "Here!" they would cry out, pointing to the broken, worn down spines. Every dead person had at least one story he or she wanted to tell. In the library, some of these stories had already been written down. The dead people knew this. They also knew their words meant nothing unless they were read.

Other dead people were looking to find a single fact, a sentence from a long-forgotten book. But they could no longer open the covers or turn the pages.

"They've lost my book!" a wild-eyed woman shouted as Cole turned into the aisle for American history. Cole didn't look away in time; the woman saw his glance and attached herself to his presence.

"It was here," she protested, "and now it's gone. Gone gone gone."

"Maybe somebody took it out?" Cole suggested hesitantly. Sometimes the dead people could be made to feel better through simple logic.

"I burned it!" the woman screeched, digging her fingers into her eyes.

Cole didn't know what she meant, or what she was going to do next. He didn't want to know. He walked away, keeping his eye on her as he retrieved the few books about the War of 1812. As soon as he had them in his hand, he retreated to a far-off desk in the reading room.

Even in the middle of the afternoon, the reading room was busy. People sat at the tables reading books and magazines, some with papers and printouts spread out in front of them, others looking like they were at their desks at home, reading under their favorite lamp. What these people didn't realize was that there were dead people reading over their shoulders, peering at the open pages, hoping to find the words that would set them free.

Cole tried to ignore their murmurs as they brought the words to life from the page, creating a great undertow of sentences that filled the library — and that only Cole could hear.

One or two dead people passed behind Cole as he read about the War of 1812. The books he had couldn't help them.

But those books *might* be able to help free Cole of John Heginbotham.

First Cole read an encyclopedia entry and learned the basics of the War of 1812. It was caused because America felt Great Britain was unjustly imprisoning its sailors, blocking its trade, and teaming up with the Indians out west. Plus, America wanted a reason to invade Canada and take more territory. President Madison declared war in 1812, and it wasn't over until 1815. During that time, the British invaded the new capitol of Washington D.C. and burned down the White House and the Capitol Building. They also tried to invade the north from Canada and the south in New Orleans, but were fought back. In the end, neither side really won — a treaty was drafted that basically made things go back to the way they were before the war.

So what role did John Heginbotham play in any of this? Cole turned to the back of each book to see if his name was in the index. Each time, it was.

Most of the books told the same story . . . and it was a very interesting story.

In 1814, John Heginbotham was arrested for treason. Washington D.C. had fallen to the British, and Baltimore looked like it would be next. A British spy was captured and confessed that the British government had been sent classified documents about the District of Columbia's defenses. The American turncoat was known only by the code name Hangman. The American army investigated and traced the leak back to Heginbotham. He was tried and quickly convicted, one of the first people in the new nation to be found guilty of treason. To set an example, Heginbotham — Hangman — was hanged. He protested his innocence, but nobody believed him. He was killed on December 17, 1814 . . . in the building that would later become Cole's school.

None of the books spent more than a page on Heginbotham. Cole flipped to the back to look at the footnotes. There he found a number of articles about Heginbotham listed. They were all by Professor David Rohlfing of the University of Pennsylvania.

The name sounded familiar to Cole, but at first he couldn't figure out why. Then he remembered: the book that had fallen at his feet in the library — the book that had shown him John Heginbotham in the first place — had been written by Rohlfing.

Cole headed to the library's periodical computer. Rohlfing's articles were listed, but none of them were in the library's collections. The librarian, a kind lady named Harriet Goldsmith, explained that they could be ordered from another library. It would take a few days to get them. Cole wasn't sure he had that much time . . . but he signed up to get the articles anyway.

The articles had been written one every few months, until they abruptly ended four years ago. Cole wondered why Rohlfing had stopped.

It was beginning to get late, and Cole had to get home soon. His mom would be annoyed if she got home before he did; right now, he was supposed to be at his desk, doing his homework like the good student he was trying to be. Although this trip to the library was *research*, it wasn't really *homework*. Nobody would ever give him a good grade for helping a dead person. No, they'd just tell him he looked too tired in class, and would fail him when he didn't have time to read the assignment before a pop quiz.

The house was quiet when Cole walked in — the familiar quiet of a house that's been empty all day. He took the War of 1812 books out of his backpack and put them on his desk. If his mom asked, he'd tell her they were for a report. He didn't want to bother her with any more.

Cole's mom knew his secret, but you couldn't really say she was happy about it. She supported Cole through thick and thin, but still thought of his gift as more of a curse. Sometimes she acted as if it had happened because of something she'd done wrong. If only she'd been a better mother, Cole wouldn't see dead people. If only Cole's dad hadn't walked out on the family, Cole wouldn't see dead people. If only she had noticed it sooner, she might have been able to stop it. Cole knew this wasn't true, but there was no way to convince his mom.

He heard her key in the front lock and came down to greet her. This was a ritual for them — whenever one of them came home, the other would be waiting just inside the door, so the house wouldn't seem at all empty.

There used to be times when Cole's mom would come into the house and she would be so happy and proud of herself. It was like the day had been a game and she'd won it.

That hadn't been happening much lately. Now when Lynn Sear came home, she looked like she'd lost the day. She tried to smile for Cole and put on a happy routine. But Cole knew her too well to fall for it. He could tell something was wrong at work. Lynn worked as an assistant to a financial consultant, and lately he'd been really on her case. "I can't do anything right," Lynn would say out of the blue, shaking her head. Cole knew she was talking about the day she'd had at work. And it was clear from the tone of her voice that she wasn't really the one who couldn't do anything right — it was her boss.

Today she looked even more tired than usual.

"I feel like there are elephants slamdancing in my head right now, honey," she explained as she headed straight for her chair in the living room. When she got there, she kicked off her shoes and closed her eyes. "How was your day?"

Sometimes Cole and his mom played a game where they would pick the most fantastic day to talk about . . . even if it wasn't at all like the day they'd really had. But you had to be in the mood to play that game. And Cole was pretty sure his mom wasn't in the mood right now.

"It was pretty good," Cole answered.

His mom's eyes remained closed. "You're lucky, then."

It was just the two of them right now. No Dad. No dead people wandering around. No immediate threat. No immediate comfort. Cole was standing a few feet from his mother, but it felt like they were at different ends of the apartment. There was comfort in knowing that there was someone else around, but there wasn't anything really to say.

Cole left to set the table. He knew his mom needed some quiet time to recover.

Sometimes dealing with living people was harder than dealing with the dead.

FOUR

That night it was Cole who was hanged.

He was sitting in English class, taking a test. He looked up and saw Jason in front of him, head bent over his paper. He looked to the front of the classroom and saw Ms. Grant watching over the room. Then he looked at the door and saw four men there, dressed like it was 1814. Their knock shattered the silence in the classroom. Ms. Grant sensed trouble. When she got to the doorway, she tried to block the men from seeing inside. Cole heard them say his name. Ms. Grant answered that he wasn't here.

The men pushed her aside and came straight to Cole's desk. He tried to scream, but a hand was over his face before he had a chance. All the other students — even Jason — looked on. Some of them seemed shocked. Others looked like they had seen this coming.

Cole was pushed out of his seat. His hands were cuffed in old wooden manacles. He was led from the class, into the hall. He tried to escape, but it was no use. As he was marched forward, his footsteps became heavier and heavier. As he passed each classroom, kids pressed against the glass windows, trying to steal a view. Finally he was led to the gym, where a gallows had been erected. It was shaped just like in a game of Hangman, only this time it was drawn in wood instead of pencil. A man in a black hood waited for him. Cole frantically looked around, hoping to find someone to help him. His mom. Detective Brown. John Heginbotham. Ms. Grant. But they were all being kept outside as Cole was marched forward, his heartbeats now as loud as the footsteps. He was walking up stairs, up to the platform . . . up to the rope.

The man in the black hood asked Cole if he had any final words. Before he could answer, the noose was lowered.

Cole felt the rope around his neck.

Then he woke up, falling through the trapdoor out of sleep.

It had seemed so real. Cole could remember it perfectly.

It was five in the morning. At least an hour before dawn. But Cole couldn't go back to sleep.

He didn't want to.

At breakfast, Cole tried to act like everything was normal. His mom seemed a little happy — for the first time in a while, she'd slept straight through the night. Cole didn't want to ruin that.

But there were some things Cole couldn't hide. As he poured the milk on his cereal, he could see his mom stopping to look at him.

"What's that on your neck?" she asked.

"Nothing," Cole answered. He didn't know what she was talking about.

She came over and pointed at something Cole couldn't see. When her finger came close, Cole flinched.

"Right there. It looks like a burn."

A rope burn.

"My shirt was scratching me yesterday," Cole explained. He knew it was a lie, and he waited for a moment to see if his mom would catch him on it. She certainly had reason to be suspicious. When the dead people got angry, they could cause bruises and cuts. But they hadn't done that in a while. So Cole hoped his mother would believe what she wanted to believe.

She looked him in the eye, and he tried hard not to look away.

I can't ruin her day. Not this early.

"We'll have to do something about that shirt," she said finally.

Cole nodded and finished his cereal.

When the bowl was rinsed out and his mom was busy looking for her keys, he stole a glance at a mirror. Sure enough, there was a red mark on the side of his neck. Right where the noose would have gripped.

He didn't know how it had gotten there. Or why.

But he knew it wasn't an accident.

He knew he wasn't even safe in his sleep.

"I'll give you a ride," Lynn called out from her bedroom. She only offered him a ride to school when she sensed something was wrong, even if she didn't know exactly what it was.

"It's okay," Cole called back. Right now, he wanted her to think everything was all right.

Even if it was a lie.

FIVE

The dream had been so real that Cole irrationally expected to see the gallows when he walked into gym class that morning. Instead he found a row of volleyball nets waiting for him. Not quite as scary — but still not safe.

Cole didn't like gym class when it was indoors. He liked it when they were outside — his mind could wander and it wouldn't matter. He liked running the best, taking off from everyone else, doing it all on his own. Last year, his teacher had told him he'd be really good at track when he was in high school. This year, the teacher thought differently. This year, the teacher was Mr. Peake, a man with a stomach the size of Cole, who sat on a sagging chair and shouted abuse at everyone but the total jocks.

Cole tried not to draw attention to himself in gym class. He made sure his T-shirt was the same white as everyone else's and that his push-ups always ended at the right time. He didn't lunge for the ball, but he didn't run away from it. Mostly, he tried to get through the forty minutes without having Mr. Peake single him out for scorn.

This wasn't always easy.

Cole changed in the locker room and moved into the gymnasium with everyone else. Up in the stands, the deranged dead man rocked back and forth. Sometimes he murmured the same word over and over again — *guilty, guilty, guilty.* Sometimes he was as silent as a stare. He didn't seem to want anything from Cole. He might not have even realized Cole was there.

The class had both older kids and younger kids. Cole saw Dennis, the bully, and some of the other kids who'd teased him in the library. Before, they hadn't known who he was. Now that had changed. Cole would have to be even less visible than usual.

Mr. Peake made them all count off and divide into teams. Cole ended up with a few of the bad kids. He thought they hadn't noticed him. Then Dennis came over and whispered, "I'm not through with you."

Cole looked away. Some of the other kids chimed

in — "Hey, it's the spaz from the library," "He still looks like his underwear's too tight," "I'll bet you're afraid of the ball!"

Cole tried to ignore them, and took his place in the volleyball lines. Dennis was standing right in front of him.

"You better be careful, or I might spike *you,*" he snarled.

Why is this happening to me? Cole wondered. It's like his *existence* offended these guys. It wasn't fair.

The game started. Cole made a good shot, then missed two.

He was so concentrated on the game that he didn't notice the air in the gymnasium shift. The other kids started to shiver in their T-shirts and gym shorts, rubbing their arms between plays, shifting from foot to foot. Mr. Peake yelled at a kid to close the windows. The kid meekly replied that the windows were already shut.

Cole looked up at the rocking dead man. But that didn't make sense — he was always in the gym, and it wasn't always cold.

Then Cole started to hear the footsteps.

No one else could hear them. No one else could feel the ground shake. They just shivered a little more; a few kids went to get sweatshirts.

Cole couldn't see anything. But he could sense it. *Behind me.*

Slowly, he turned. John Heginbotham's blood-drowned eyes were staring at him intently, the rope frayed around his neck. He opened his mouth in a cry, but no real sound came out. Just a silent gagging, like choking on sand.

Cole jumped back, knocking into another kid. One of the boys from the library.

"Hey, watch it, spaz," the boy spat out.

The dead man stepped forward. From the other side of the net, a girl served the volleyball.

You are going to help me, Heginbotham's expression said. *You are going to help me . . . or else.*

The ball arched over the net. Cole saw it coming toward him, but had lost his ability to think. He was paralyzed. The other boys were yelling at him. He saw the ball coming his way. Heginbotham began to pull the rope around his own neck, causing his flesh to burn red. Cole held out his arms. He caught the ball.

"What are you doing?" the kid he'd knocked into yelled.

The game stopped. People were staring at him.

"Let go of the ball!" Mr. Peake yelled.

"Go away," Cole told the hanged man. "Leave me alone."

35

"What did he say?" Mr. Peake hollered from his seat.

"He said for you to go away," one of the boys from the library said.

"He called you a name," another boy answered.

"I did not!" Cole protested.

"Yeah, he called you a lard!" the first boy shouted out.

"He called you something worse," Dennis chimed in.

"He's a spaz."

"He won't let go of the ball!"

"They're lying," a girl on Cole's team protested, and other girls backed her up. But Mr. Peake wouldn't listen to them. He never listened to girls.

He was so angry he almost got out of his chair. But not quite.

"I think someone here has an attitude problem," he grunted.

The boy Cole had collided with reached over to pull the ball out of his hands. At the same time, Heginbotham reached out to grab Cole. Cole stumbled back and ran into the kid again. This time the kid pushed back, cheered on by Dennis and the others.

Mr. Peake blew the whistle he always wore around his neck.

"Enough!" he shouted. Cole stopped, but the other kid didn't. He gave Cole one last shove, which sent him falling to the floor. The ball dropped from his hands and he landed on his backside.

"Freak," one of the boys hissed. Other kids started saying it too.

"Go to the office!" Mr. Peake commanded. At first, Cole thought he was talking to the kid who'd pushed him. But no — he was only talking to Cole.

Heginbotham retreated. The girl who'd defended Cole reached out to give him a hand. Mr. Peake yelled at her to get back in her place. She kept her hand out and Cole took it, even though it embarrassed him.

"We're not doing a thing until you leave for the office, Mr. Sear!" Mr. Peake stormed from his chair.

"You better go," the girl whispered. "I wish I could come with you. Anywhere's better than here."

Cole didn't know her name. He started to move for the locker room.

"No changing!" Mr. Peake said. "You're to go straight to the office."

Cole couldn't believe the other boy wasn't being sent, too. Or, even worse, he *could* believe it. He could believe that life would be so unfair.

He walked in his gym clothes to the principal's

office, Heginbotham's footsteps close at his heels. He didn't turn around; he didn't want to see what the hanged man was up to.

The principal was only slightly surprised to see Cole. He hadn't been in the principal's office for a while, but before that he'd been in situations like this all the time. There was no way for him to explain his behavior. So he'd gotten into trouble until he'd found a way to control his reactions — and prevent the dead people from ruining his life.

Now it was happening again.

Mr. Peake had called the office from the gym and had given an account — a totally biased, unfair account — of what had happened.

"You called Mr. Peake a lard and told him to go away?" the principal asked. Even though it wasn't true, Cole couldn't think of a way to deny it.

Then things got worse. John Heginbotham came into the room and began to scrape at the walls. Cole focused on him, wondering what he'd do next.

"Are you listening to me?" the principal asked. Cole didn't hear him until he'd repeated it twice. The principal was not amused by this. He was studying Cole closely.

"I will not tolerate outbursts like this in my school," he said. "You have always been skating on thin ice here, just one straw short of breaking the

38

camel's back. I will admit that I haven't heard your name as much these past few months. But that doesn't mean you can start acting the way you used to. Going to this school is a privilege. I don't think you understand that. I'm going to have to call your mother."

This got Cole's attention.

"No!" he said instinctively. His mom had enough trouble as it was. If she thought he was having problems in school again, she'd flip.

"Yes," the principal said. "I think we need to nip this one in the bud before the molehill turns into a mountain. I think it's time for us all to have another conference. What's your mother's number at work?"

Cole knew his mom got into trouble with her boss for any phone calls that didn't have to do with her job. But he didn't see how he could lie to the principal. So he wrote down the number . . . and prayed the principal wouldn't actually call.

As he handed over the phone number, Heginbotham leaned over to look at it. Cole tried to cover it with his hand. The principal misunderstood this, thinking Cole was trying to hide the number from *him*. He snatched the piece of paper from Cole's hand and gestured at him to leave.

"Go change," he said. "You shouldn't be walking around the school in those clothes."

I know. It wasn't my choice, Cole thought. But what could he say?

As Cole walked out of the office, he turned back and could see the principal dialing the numbers on the piece of paper.

"Hello, Mrs. Sear . . ."

Cole left before he could hear any more.

He already knew the bottom line:

He was in big trouble.

SIX

Cole was in no hurry to get home after school. Instead, he headed to the school library. He kept his head low as he walked through the halls — he didn't want any of the bullies to see him. He hated walking this way . . . but he didn't have any choice. He wasn't about to take them on, so it was best to just avoid them.

He made it to the library without being spotted.

Ms. Larkin was shelving books when he arrived. The rest of the library was empty. As usual, there weren't any dead people around in the new addition.

Cole knew he had to track down more information about John Heginbotham — but how? None of the books had been able to help him. And the hanged man clearly was unable to speak for himself. His voice box had probably been crushed by the rope.

Then Cole remembered — Professor Rohlfing.

If Rohlfing had written articles about John Heginbotham, he might know even more about why he was hanged. It was a long shot, but Cole didn't see any close shots to take.

He went over to the phone book; there weren't any Rohlfings listed.

Cole immediately wanted to give up. This was *so stupid*, trying to solve a two-hundred-year-old mystery in order to make a dead man go away. How was he supposed to handle this? All by himself?

Ms. Larkin came over to ask Cole if there was anything he needed.

"Do you have any old phone books?" he asked.

She looked at him curiously, but didn't ask him why he needed an old phone book. "I'm afraid we throw the old ones away," she said kindly.

Cole sighed and threw his backpack on. He might as well go home and face his mom when she got home. . . .

"Wait!" Ms. Larkin called out, raising her hand after Cole. "I just thought of something."

She led Cole back into the Periodical Room, where all the old magazines were kept in haphazard stacks. In the back of the room there was a cluttered wood table; underneath one of its legs, there was an old telephone book propping it up.

"That's been there for at least five years," Ms. Larkin said. "Will that work?"

Cole nodded. As Ms. Larkin held up the table, he slipped out the telephone book and replaced it with a stack of old magazines.

"I'll put it back," Cole promised.

Ms. Larkin left him alone in the Periodical Room. Cole quickly flipped through the columns of names until he had gotten to the R's.

There it was:

D. ROHLFING   19 EXETER ROW   555-7216

Exeter Row was only a few blocks away from the school.

Cole now knew where he was going next.

Cole's school was in a borderline area of town. On the one side were the crowded, citylike apartments where normal working people lived, like Cole and his mom. On the other side was a nicer area, with big houses and private parking spaces and front gates. Some of the houses had been lived in by the same families for centuries. Others housed people from the government or the university.

The house at 19 Exeter Row was big and fore-boding. It was an old Victorian house, with two floors and an elaborate gate. It should have looked wealthy and impressive, but instead it looked empty and sad. The paint was peeling in places, and the front yard was overgrown with weeds. It was the kind of house that would remain dark even on Halloween; visitors clearly weren't welcome. Cole almost turned around without knocking. Then he remembered John Heginbotham's face coming close to his, and he found himself slowly walking up the steps. The front gate was dangling open.

Cole rang the doorbell, but he didn't hear any corresponding sound from outside. He pressed the button again and listened closer. Still no sound. He rang a third time, holding the button down, struggling to hear if the doorbell worked at all. Suddenly, a voice hollered, "All right already!" Cole jumped back as the door opened abruptly.

"Are you trying to wake the dead?" the man answering the door asked. He was about sixty years old, from what Cole could tell, and looked like he'd just woken up.

"I'm sorry," Cole apologized. "I'm looking for —"

"Look," the man interrupted, "I don't want to buy anything you have to sell, or hear anything you have to say. I don't want any subscriptions to magazines

I'll never read, I don't want to buy any tickets for raffles I'll never win, and I don't have the money to help your team or troop go to wherever it is you need to go."

"But —"

"I'm afraid there's no 'but' here. I see you're on the young side, so I'm trying not to be too harsh. You're not a salesman, and thank God for that. But I'll give you some advice for free — selling things door to door is not a very healthy profession, especially when you get to this door. So it would be best for everyone involved if you turn around right now and close the gate behind you. Whatever it is, I'm not interested."

Cole knew he only had one more chance to get a word in. Quickly he said, "Professor Rohlfing, I came to ask you about John Heginbotham."

Now it was Professor Rohlfing who was momentarily struck speechless. He gave Cole a long, hard look and then shook his head.

"What do you know about John Heginbotham?" he asked in a steely voice.

"I know he was hanged during the War of 1812 in my school, back when it was used for hanging people. I know he said he was innocent. I know you wrote a lot about him, but I can't get copies of your articles from the library because they have to be ordered in from somewhere else." Cole had to stop himself short before adding, *I've actually seen John Heginbotham and I know he wants something from me, and possibly from you, too. But I don't know what . . .*

Professor Rohlfing looked over his shoulder at the dark interior of his house, as if checking to see if it was okay to open the door. Finally he must have been reassured by what he'd seen (or what he hadn't seen), since he opened the door further and motioned Cole to come inside.

"This way," he said, leading Cole into a murky living room, every wall covered with shelves of books. "Is this for a school project?"

"Yes," Cole lied. It was much easier than telling the truth.

"And how did you find me?"

"Someone at the university told me." It seemed like a better answer than *I looked you up in an old phone book.*

"Good. Very good."

Cole could see what Professor Rohlfing was like in front of a classroom, pacing and deliberating before he said his next statement in definitive tones.

"Not many people remember John Heginbotham nowadays," he began in earnest. "He's become a footnote figure in a footnote war. Do you know what

I mean by that? Basically, it means that nobody cares about the War of 1812 anymore. Compared to the World Wars, it seems very minor — two countries squabbling over shipping rights, each one trying to take over more land, but in the end going back to the way things were before the war started. Not very fascinating. And although John Heginbotham was one of the first people hanged for treason in this country, people don't really care about him either. This is partially because there's so little documentation left; nobody knows the whole story, and most people think the whole story is the only one worth telling. I disagree."

As Professor Rohlfing talked, Cole could hear a rocking noise over his head, the sound of something hitting roundly against the other side of the ceiling. Then, as Professor Rohlfing finished, there was a loud crash from a totally different part of the second floor, followed by an audible cry.

Professor Rohlfing's expression suddenly turned pained.

"I'm afraid you're going to have to leave," he said, practically lifting Cole out of his chair.

"But I haven't gotten a chance to —" Cole began to protest.

"*Not now,*" Professor Rohlfing said emphatically.

"Can I come back?"

"Yes, yes. Just not right now."

The crying had stopped, but Professor Rohlfing still wanted Cole out. Cole thought his behavior was strange, but couldn't think of a way to say so. Instead, he allowed the older man to lead him outside, slamming the door at his back. He walked down the front path and regarded the house again from a distance.

He looked at the upstairs windows and saw a woman looking out from one of them. Her hair was dark, her features blurry behind a screen. As soon as she saw him, she let the curtain fall, retreating into the room.

Cole waited for a moment, wondering if she'd come back. But the curtain remained closed. The house remained quiet. It was still afternoon, but Cole felt a darkness within him.

He was sure Professor Rohlfing could help him unravel the mystery of the hanged man.

But he wasn't sure whether Professor Rohlfing *would* help him.

Professor Rohlfing had things of his own to deal with.

SEVEN

There was a message on the answering machine when Cole got home from Professor Rohlfing's house. It was from Cole's mom.

"I'm going to be working late tonight. Your principal called and I have to go in to see him tomorrow morning during work time. I don't care how late I'm home, I want you to be ready to give me a full explanation. I'll call again if it's going to be past your bedtime."

Cole knew it was possible to love someone and be mad at him at the same time. Both his mom and his dad had been very good at that, until the point where they had stopped being in love and were only mad all the time. Ever since Cole had started to get a grip on his sixth sense, his mom had never really been angry with him. He hoped that wouldn't start to change now.

Cole didn't like eating dinner alone. Even if he turned the TV on — which he wasn't allowed to do when his mom was home for dinner — the house still seemed lonely. Seven o'clock came and he finished his frozen pizza. Eight o'clock came and he finished his homework. Nine o'clock came and his favorite TV show was over. Usually he and his mom would argue about whether or not it had been a good episode. But she'd missed it tonight. And she hadn't called.

By nine-thirty, Cole was exhausted. By ten, he was in bed.

He fell into a dreamless, nightmareless almost-sleep. Then he sensed someone watching him, breathing darkly in his room.

He opened his eyes and saw the red light of the clock: 11:12.

Then he saw his mom, silently hanging back in the doorway.

"Are you awake?" she asked.

"Uh-huh," Cole replied.

She came over to his bed.

"I'm sorry I'm so late. Mr. Richardson was running me ragged, putting together this report for tomorrow. Dora and I were in his office the whole time, finishing his stupid graphs. I tried to sneak out to my desk to call you, but he told me to stay. He said it would only be another half hour, and that was three hours ago. Plus, I have to go to your school tomorrow morning, which he was *not* happy about. But what can I do? At least he pays overtime."

"I know," Cole whispered.

"Now what's this about getting into trouble in gym class?"

Cole could tell she wasn't that angry — just tired and confused. So he told her the whole story . . . well, most of it. He didn't give her details about Heginbotham, just told her there was a dead person in the gym. He told her about what the other bullies had done, and how the one girl had stood up for him. He told her how awful Mr. Peake was, and she nodded sympathetically.

"Okay then," she said. "We'll just have to get through this conference tomorrow. They'll never understand you, Cole. Nobody ever will. We'll have to find a way to get them off your back without telling them everything. Right?"

"Right."

"But listen to me, okay? You have to be extra careful at a private school like yours. Even if it's not your fault, you can't get into trouble. The people who don't understand you will want to get rid of you

51

because they can't understand you. You can't give them any reasons, Cole, or else you're playing right into their hands."

"It's not fair!" Cole protested quietly.

Lynn pulled Cole into a hug. "I know," she said, rocking him gently. "Believe me, I know."

They were quiet at breakfast the next morning, each thinking about the conference. Cole hadn't slept well and was trying to hide his jittery nerves. He was surprised to find Ms. Grant, Mr. Peake, and Ms. Keller (his guidance counselor) waiting in the principal's office when they arrived.

"I've asked some of your teachers here to discuss your behavior," the principal said. Then, as an afterthought, he added, "Thank you for coming, Mrs. Sear."

Cole could see his mom taking it all in. She knew what he had already figured out — that this conference wasn't just about the gym incident. This was a conference about him in general.

"Cole is one of my star students," Ms. Grant began. "He's shown remarkable improvement in the past few months, and is a fine writer." She turned to Lynn and said, "He's a pleasure to have in class."

Cole could see his mom was a little surprised by this. Surprised and pleased. She used to come home from parent-teacher conferences looking defeated; year after year, the teachers would say the same things — *"Cole is always distracted," "Cole is a slow learner," "Cole has an erratic temper," "Cole doesn't have many friends."* Now a teacher was actually saying *good* things about him. Cole was psyched, especially since he liked Ms. Grant so much.

The principal didn't seem as impressed. "Mr. Peake?" he intoned.

"I'm afraid I disagree," Mr. Peake said. He still sagged in the chair, but he'd taken off his whistle for this visit to the main office. "I think Cole is a troublemaker who needs to be disciplined. He picks fights with other children, calls teachers names, and doesn't follow the rules."

"That's not true!" Cole protested.

Mr. Peake didn't even turn to look at Cole, instead focusing on the principal. "The boy caught a volleyball and held on to it. That's what I call not following the rules."

Cole was sure his mother would have something to say to that, but instead it was Ms. Grant who spoke up.

"With all due respect to my *colleague*," she said, "that has not been my experience at all with Cole, and I believe his other teachers would back me up. I've fumbled a few volleyballs in my day, but that doesn't make me a bad student. I think we should be congratulating Cole on his improvement, not chastising him for one incident that was clearly a case of miscommunication between Cole and his gym teacher."

Cole watched his mom to see what her reaction would be, but she was holding back, taking it all in.

Ms. Keller spoke for the first time. "I agree, Lauren. But I'm afraid we have to take this incident in the greater context. Both the principal and I are afraid that Cole is returning to his . . . old behavior, which you weren't here to see. We don't want to see him slipping back to his old ways."

"You're right," Ms. Grant said. "I didn't know Cole back then. But if he's doing okay now, I don't see what that has to do with anything."

"He's a troublemaker!" Mr. Peake piped in. "I've seen it with my own eyes."

Lynn Sear couldn't stay quiet any longer. "And when my son was pushed to the ground by another kid, did you see *that* with your own eyes?" she asked. "When he was teased, when these boys lied and said that he'd called you a name, did you see any of that with your own eyes? It appears to me that you have very selective vision."

"Now, look here, little lady —" Mr. Peake sputtered.

"Don't you dare call me little lady, you little man," Lynn interrupted. "And don't you dare tell me you know anything about my son."

"Now Ms. Sear —" the principal interjected.

As they argued about what had happened in gym, Cole heard the footsteps approach. He felt the cold. He felt the hanged man's presence.

"Tell me which kids pushed you!" Mr. Peake insisted. "You're making that up."

Cole wasn't about to name names — it would only get him into more trouble, especially if he brought Dennis into it. So he said he didn't know their names, and watched as John Heginbotham began to circle the office, studying each of the adults in the room with Cole.

"Whatever the case," the principal said, "in order for us to rest easy and sleep tight, we need reassurances that Cole will behave while he is a student at this school."

"I don't think that's necessary," Ms. Grant said.

"I think it is," Ms. Keller argued.

Heginbotham took note of the principal's suit, the guidance counselor's gold watch, an earring that dangled from Ms. Grant's ear. Then he came to Cole's mom and stayed still. Watching. Observing. Taking her all in.

No, Cole thought. *Please leave her alone.*

The dead people had never bothered Cole's mom before. They had haunted their apartment, wrecked their furniture, caused chaos wherever Cole went. But they had never lifted a hand against Lynn. They had never taken any interest in her.

But now Heginbotham was reaching out for her hair. Lynn shivered from the cold and pulled her jacket tighter around her. The gnarled hand was about to rub against the back of her neck, tracing down her spine. . . .

Cole jumped from his chair. Heginbotham, startled, pulled away.

"Cole?" the principal asked. Even Lynn shot Cole a look, asking him what was going on.

How could he explain?

"Sorry," he mumbled, sitting back down.

"This is *exactly* what I mean," Ms. Keller said. "How long before the other things start again? The crying out in class, the fights with other kids, the constant inattention to his studies, the loss of friends? How long before we are in here again, asking questions but not getting any answers? How long before something serious happens?"

"Look," Lynn Sear said, "my son is okay. You've heard it from his English teacher. You're hearing it from me. Cole is doing great. All his grades are up. All his teacher comments are good. He has friends.

He's happy. If you want, I'm sure he will apologize for catching a volleyball or allowing himself to be pushed to the ground or whatever it is that offended Mr. Peake. But I don't think we need to be making a big deal about this. He's doing great."

The principal leaned back in his chair. "I understand all that," he said. "And certainly what Ms. Grant has said is being taken into account. So we're not going to make more of this than necessary. I'm glad we all know where we stand. Cole's behavior has been improving, and none of us want to see him take any steps backward. That's what we're saying."

But Cole knew what they were really saying: *Watch yourself. Because if you act like this again, we're not going to be as understanding.*

It was clear from the principal's posture that the conference was at an end. Lynn made a point of thanking Ms. Grant as they walked out into the hall. Ms. Grant said it was nothing — Cole really was a pleasure to have in class. Cole nearly blushed at that, but kept it in (he thought).

When they were alone together, Cole's mom let out a big sigh.

"You watch out for yourself, okay?" she said to Cole before heading to her car.

"I will," Cole replied. Other kids were walking around them, watching them say good-bye.

Lynn saw him looking at them and laughed. "Don't worry," she said. "I won't hug you in front of the whole school."

"Thanks, Mom," Cole mumbled, smiling.

Lynn looked at her watch. "God, I'm late. Let's hope that Mr. Richardson's awful, awful wife kept him late this morning, so he won't notice."

With that and another good-bye, she was off to her car. Cole felt good for another minute or so. Then, on his way to class, Ms. Keller's words came back to him.

How long before the other things start again? The crying out in class, the fights with other kids, the constant inattention to his studies, the loss of friends? How long before we are in here again, asking questions but not getting any answers? How long before something serious happens?

Cole had thought he could handle the dead people. He'd thought he could be in control. But now he wasn't sure any more. He'd thought all that stuff — the crying, the screaming, the lack of focus — was over. But what if it wasn't?

How long would he last?

EIGHT

The rest of the day was a nightmare. Cole had suspected that Mr. Peake wasn't exactly going to be nice to him from now on, but he hadn't realized how low the gym teacher would stoop. Besides assigning him extra sit-ups during warm-up and making loud comments about the state of Cole's gym clothes (which looked clean enough to Cole), Mr. Peake also decided to make an "announcement" to the rest of the class.

"As you know," he said, "we had a bit of a disturbance yesterday in this class. The person who was responsible for the disturbance tried to blame it on other people, but I wouldn't let him. So let this be a warning; some of your fellow students are to be trusted more than others."

Cole didn't know what to do. He was being called

a liar and a tattletale. And there wasn't a single way for him to protest without getting into more trouble.

The girl who'd helped him yesterday seemed as indignant as Cole.

"I can't believe it," she said. "I was here. I saw it. He's the one who's lying."

"Do I hear conversation over there?" Mr. Peake yelled. "Split it up, you two. You're no longer on the same team."

None of the guys who'd picked on Cole came right out and picked on him again during class. No, they were more subtle about it. They let the ball come his way, even when he was nowhere in position to hit it back, so he would be the one to lose the point. Kids on the other side spiked the ball his way; when it was his time to serve, he felt an enormous pressure to do well, which meant he was so nervous that he kept serving it out-of-bounds.

Cole expected some sort of retaliation in the locker room after class. But kids kept their distance. Cole let down his guard, relieved. He packed up his gym clothes and approached the hallway.

They were waiting for him there.

There were five or six of them, all bigger than Cole.

"What's the matter, spaz?" one jeered. "Your mommy not here to help you now?"

Cole kicked out, trying to free himself. But they

only laughed at him, grabbing his arms, pulling him forward.

"Come on, we've got a place for tattletales like you."

They were approaching the old janitor's closet. Cole sensed something disturbing inside — something even the bullies couldn't know about.

"No!" he cried out. Again, he got laughter in return.

Dennis's voice came across loud and clear. "You should've thought about this before you picked a fight with us," he said. "If you're good, maybe we'll let you out at the end of the day."

The door to the janitor's closet was open. Cole was pushed inside. The door was shut again.

Cole tried to open it from the inside.

It had been jammed.

He pressed against the door, wondering whether to yell. If he was caught in here, the principal would say that Ms. Keller had been right all along — things were back the way they used to be. But if he didn't get help, he'd be stuck in here all day, missing all his classes. He ran his fingers along the lock, under the door, trying to figure a way out.

Then he realized he wasn't alone.

He felt something push against his spine. His blood ran cold.

"You're in my way," a voice said.

Cole turned.

It was a horrific sight.

All the man's hair had been charred off — even his eyebrows. His skin was burned and boiled. The fingers of his hand were fused together. He was holding a broom. He jabbed the end of it toward Cole's neck.

"Get out of my way!" he yelled. "I'm trying to clean."

Cole remembered a story about a janitor a few years before. A smoker who one night fell asleep before he'd put his cigarette out. His bed caught fire. He hadn't died instantly, but eventually he'd died.

And now he was here. Doing his old job.

Nothing would stand in his way.

He removed the broom from Cole's neck and swept at his feet.

"MOVE!" he screamed. Cole tried to move, but there wasn't any room.

Now the janitor was angry.

Some dead people were like this. All they wanted was to keep at their old routine. They would never find peace because they would never find rest. They would destroy anything that came in their way.

Cole pressed himself into a corner. The dead janitor began to push at him with the hard end of the broom. Cole could feel the pressure against his chest. He could feel the bruise beginning to form.

"Let me out!" he yelled, lunging for the door, pounding at the door. He didn't care what the principal thought or anybody else thought. He had to be safe.

He heard footsteps on the other side of the door. The flick of the lock. The door opening.

Cole was blinded by the sudden shot of light. It took him a second to recognize the girl from his gym class.

He saw her look him over, dirty and sweaty, his shirt torn. He saw her look at the rest of the closet. But of course all she could see were the janitorial supplies.

"I'm sorry it took me so long," she said. "I saw them get you, but then they waited here for a couple of minutes to make sure you couldn't get out. I came as soon as they left."

For an instant, Cole found himself hating her. Not for waiting for so long, but for showing up at all. She had saved him, and he didn't want to have to be saved. He wanted to face this on his own. He knew she wouldn't always be there. But the dead people would be.

"Thanks," he said weakly. Then, when he realized how cold he sounded, he added, "Thanks a lot."

She looked at him seriously. "You're strange, aren't you?"

"I guess."

"Don't worry. That's a good thing." She held out her hand. "I'm Riley."

"Riley?"

"It's my last name. But everybody calls me that."

"What's your first name?" Cole asked, shaking her hand, feeling a little silly for doing it.

"I'm not telling. And we're both late for class. So I guess I'll see you around."

Before Cole could say another word, she dashed off. Maybe she was as embarrassed as he was. But she didn't seem embarrassed. It was all very confusing.

Cole closed the door of the janitor's closet and headed to class, stopping first into the bathroom to clean himself off.

He expected an attack from Dennis and the other bullies later in the day, but somehow he managed to avoid them. After school, he walked over to Professor Rohlfing's house, hoping to continue their conversation about John Heginbotham. But this time the gate was locked and nobody answered the bell. Cole looked at the house, searching for the movement of a curtain or the glow of a light. But there were no signs of life. Cole was out of luck.

At home that night, Lynn was really tense. She didn't say anything more about the conference, or anything at all about her day at work. Cole could tell it had been really bad. He couldn't think of any way to make it that much better.

His nightmares grew more intense. He saw himself hanged. His mother hanged. His friends hanged. Even Riley appeared in the nightmares — only when she appeared, the hangings stopped. She would take him away from the gallows. She would save him again and again.

Over the next few days, he saw her a few times, in gym class and outside of it, but they never talked. She was only a year older than him — not that big a difference — but it was enough that they didn't have any classes or even lunch together.

Cole saw John Heginbotham instead. He saw John Heginbotham *all the time*. He felt that the hanged man was trying to tell him something . . . but he couldn't speak. There wasn't even a way for him to spell things about. Sometimes he'd point to his shoes, but Cole didn't know what this meant. He'd guess the wrong things, which would only make the dead man more frustrated — and angry.

As a result, Cole was losing sleep, losing his appetite, and losing his patience. Little noises made him jump. His clothes always felt too tight — especially around his neck. Every day, Cole would walk over to Professor Rohlfing's house after school. Every day, no one would answer. Cole started to sense someone inside . . . but nobody would come to the window or the door.

A few days after the janitor's closet incident, Cole had another run-in with Dennis. Cole was at his locker when the bully came over. This time, they were both alone.

"We're not through with you yet," Dennis snarled.

Cole knew he had to stay calm.

"DID YOU HEAR ME?" Dennis shouted. Cole's books dropped to the floor.

Other kids in the hall were watching now.

Cole felt the urge to fight back. Why did he have to take this? What was stopping him from being just as aggressive as Dennis and the other kids?

Back in the old days, back when everyone thought he was a freak, at least they'd been afraid of him. They kept their distance because they didn't know what he'd do next.

What if it was like that again? What if he could scare them all away?

Cole was tempted. Then he thought of Jason. And Ms. Grant. And his mom. And even Riley. He would scare *them* away, too. He would prove Ms. Keller right.

How long before we are in here again, asking questions but not getting any answers? How long before something serious happens?

So he stood there. He stood there when Dennis uttered one last threat before walking away. He stood there in gym class while Mr. Peake yelled at him, and kids he didn't know spiked the ball at him. He stood there as John Heginbotham haunted his every move. He stood there as his mother stayed up all night, wanting to quit her job, but sticking with it in order to send Cole to this private school that would never understand him.

How long could he stand there, letting all these things happen? How long before all the anger and sadness and silence that he'd fought off returned again?

Any minute. It felt like that breaking point was right ahead of him . . . waiting.

NINE

The weekend brought a pause from the tension of the week. Then, on Monday, Professor Rohlfing finally opened his door again.

"Ah," he said, looking down at Cole, "it's you."

Instead of inviting Cole inside, he suggested that they take a walk.

Cole didn't care where they talked, as long as he found out more about John Heginbotham. As they were walking away, Professor Rohlfing took one last look at his house, then turned the corner. A few blocks later, they found a park bench to sit on.

"You are right in saying John Heginbotham proclaimed his innocence," Rohlfing said, sounding like a teacher. "By all accounts — and I must admit there are very few that have survived — he insisted he was an innocent man. But nobody listened to him. Which I find very interesting.

"You have to realize that this was only three decades after the Revolutionary War; many of the major figures of the time had been around for that war. Some even still had a soft spot for the British. Government was much smaller than it is now, and much more personal. Everybody knew everybody. And, tellingly, John Heginbotham knew them all.

"Whether or not Heginbotham was really guilty, all of his old friends *thought* he was guilty. And whether or not they supported the war — many legislators from this part of the country didn't — they no doubt felt *betrayed* by his actions. Here they were, trying to build a nation unlike any other nation that had built before. And one of their closest compatriots was a *spy.*

"Heginbotham had never been a particularly nice man. He was not charming like Jefferson, or brilliant like Madison. And that hurt him. People were not sad to see him fall.

"The hanging should have been a big deal in American history, like the Burr–Hamilton duel. But instead it was played down. The nation's leaders were embarrassed by it. One of their own had gone bad. They didn't want to highlight that, especially in the middle of a war they were losing."

Cole tried to take all this information in. But Professor Rohlfing still hadn't answered the most important question.

"Do you think he was innocent?" Cole asked.

The professor sighed. "Yes, I think he was innocent. But can I prove it? I'm afraid the answer's no. It's not as easy as simply saying, *Oh, he didn't do it.* No, if you want to prove he didn't do it, you should be ready to say who *did* do it. That's where I hit my dead end. There was a fire in the British archives sometime at the end of the nineteenth century, so there's no record of Heginbotham there. And the Philadelphia archives are a scattered mess. Heginbotham had no wife or children, so no one kept his papers. His friends had all abandoned him. They were convinced he was the Hangman spy. Not a kind word for him in any of their letters after his death. Such a tragedy."

"But you looked for evidence?" Cole said, trying to keep Professor Rohlfing talking.

"Yes," the older man said with a definitive nod. "I looked. I wanted a biography of Heginbotham to be my next work. I researched it as deeply as I could and wrote some articles. Then I had to stop."

Cole knew better than to ask why. Clearly, Rohlfing had his own reasons, and he wasn't about to explain them to an eleven-year-old kid.

Cole had plenty more questions to ask. But the professor looked at his watch and stood abruptly.

"I'm afraid I have to go back," he said. "I hope this all helps you with your paper. Please remember to footnote me whenever possible."

"I still need your help," Cole replied.

"Certainly." Rohlfing was in a hurry now. He didn't even say good-bye.

Cole felt he'd learned some things, but he hadn't learned nearly enough. Even if the guy *was* innocent — how could Cole possibly prove it?

At this rate, the hanged man would never go away.

Cole walked home, passing by his school on the way. Cole's mom used to ask neighborhood kids to walk Cole back and forth from school; finally, Cole had been able to convince her he was okay on his own. He sometimes missed his escorts, though. Not because they were his friends (they weren't), but because they usually distracted him from his thoughts.

Cole knew the way home from school so well that he could probably walk it with his eyes closed. But even with his eyes closed, he would still shiver when he passed 1473 Tidewater Street.

He couldn't have been older than eight when it had happened. He was in third grade, being walked home by an older kid named Dave Caplan, who was in sixth grade and an okay guy. As they turned onto Tidewater Street that day, they immediately heard the sirens. Dave wanted a closer look.

Cole was curious, too, so he went along. There was an ambulance outside the house at 1473, paramedics rushing inside with their equipment, neighbors gathering on the lawn. Out of the corner of his eye, Cole saw an old lady standing in the garden, walking over a row of flowers. Nobody else paid any attention to her. She looked up at Cole with glass-blue eyes. He moved closer to hear what she had to say. When he got close enough, she leaned over and whispered, *At last.*

Cole didn't know what she meant. There was a commotion by the door as the stretcher was rushed out of the house. Cole turned to look and when he turned back, the old lady was gone. The flowers she had been stepping on stood straight up. The paramedics rushed the stretcher into the ambulance. Cole peered through the chaos and saw the old lady lying there. And at once, from two simple words, he knew all he needed to know: she'd been really sick. She was ready to go. And so she had died.

At last.

She wasn't the first dead person he'd seen, or even the first dead person he remembered. But she was the first dead person to get through to him, to look into his eyes and find something there. Now, every time he passed the house, he thought of her. There was a new family living there now, a new family with young kids who liked to play in the garden. Cole thought the old lady would be happy about that.

He was still thinking about her when he got home. For a moment, he didn't realize there was a police car waiting out front. He was worried for a second, then he recognized Detective Brown sitting on the front step. Detective Brown wasn't exactly Cole's *friend* — Cole wasn't sure he could be friends with someone his mom's age — but he and Detective Brown definitely got along well. Detective Brown's brother had also been able to see dead people, but he hadn't been able to deal with it too well. So he'd run away, and Detective Brown had never heard from him again.

Cole was happy to see him. He also wondered why he'd come.

"There you are," the detective said when he caught sight of Cole. "I was afraid I'd be here all night."

"I had to research a report," Cole explained, thinking this wasn't exactly a lie.

"Sounds good to me. It's a nice afternoon, good to be outside."

Cole sat down next to Detective Brown on the stoop. His hat was on at its usual angle, shadowing his dark skin.

"I'll bet you're wondering why I'm here," Detective Brown said.

Cole nodded.

"Well, I won't lie to you, Cole. I won't say I was just in the neighborhood and happened to stop by. Your mom called me and wanted me to talk to you, man to man. It sounds like you've been having some hard times lately. And even though she'd never admit it to me in a million years, it sounds like your mom hasn't been having it easy, either. I bet that's hard on you, too."

Cole could see the concern in Detective Brown's eyes. Before, Cole had been involved in the cases he'd been investigating. Now there wasn't anything professional about their talk. This was purely off the record. Detective Brown wasn't coming as a detective, but as a friend of the family.

Cole mentioned a little about what has happening at school, and a lot about what was happening with his mom and her job. These were the things he couldn't talk about with his mom herself, since they all involved her. He didn't want her to think he was worried. But he was.

"I want to help her," Cole admitted.

"I hear you," Detective Brown said sympathetically. "And I'm sure you do help her, without realizing it. You think you're the man of the house now, right?"

Cole nodded.

"Well, I'll tell you something, Cole — you're *not* the man of the house, and nobody — not even your mom — expects you to be. You are the son of the house, which is a very important thing. You have to support your mother and make her laugh and help her out. But you're not the *man* of the house. You can't do everything that your dad used to do, or was supposed to do. You can't take on his share of the load. Not when it comes to money or even when it comes to keeping your mom happy. Don't expect that from yourself. Don't put yourself under that pressure."

How many times had Cole been told, "You're the man of the house now"? His mom had said it, and a lot of her friends had said it after his dad had left to be with another woman. But now Detective Brown was telling him the opposite. Or, if not exactly the opposite, then something different. And it sounded right, but not all the way right. He knew he wasn't the man of the house like his father had been. He knew he didn't have that responsibility. But at the same time, he felt like he couldn't burden his mom in the way he might have if his dad had still been around. He didn't want to add to her hard time.

He wanted to explain this to Detective Brown, but couldn't find the words. And also — he was just realizing this now — he didn't feel like burdening Detective Brown, either. He knew the detective cared about him — but how far could they really go? If Cole thought telling Detective Brown about the hanged man could somehow help make Heginbotham go away, he might give it a try. But what could Detective Brown do? This wasn't a police investigation. It was a case over two hundred years old.

"What is it, Cole?" Detective Brown asked, seeing him lost in thought.

"Nothing," Cole instinctively answered.

The detective shook his head. "It's not nothing, Cole. I can tell that."

Cole stayed quiet. He'd let Detective Brown guess. If he guessed right, they would talk about it. If he guessed wrong, that would be that.

Detective Brown gave him a reassuring pat on the back. "I know you're worried about your mom, but it's going to be okay."

It wasn't a totally wrong guess, but it wasn't totally right, either. Cole was a little sad and a little relieved that Detective Brown couldn't tell everything about him.

Being on his own meant he wouldn't have to burden anyone else.

But it also meant he was on his own when the dead people came.

TEN

Later that night, Jason called to see what was going on.

"You've seemed a little out of it lately," he said to Cole.

You haven't been sleeping. You haven't been eating. You've been losing touch with reality.

Even if Jason didn't mean these things, Cole knew they were true.

When Cole got to school the next day, he found his locker had been decorated by the bullies.

SPAZ. FREAK. LOSER.

All the old words, written in new paint. Blood red, drips frozen by drying.

Cole looked at it and didn't really feel a thing.

It was happening all over again.

Why bother washing it off? It would only reappear.

Luckily, Jason didn't feel the same way. The minute he saw what had been done to Cole's locker, he ran to the rest room and came back with an armful of wet paper towels. He started scrubbing right away, cursing at the guys who'd done it. Cole helped him clean up.

"We could have Ted beat them up," Jason suggested, mentioning his older brother. Cole tried to picture it — a sixteen-year-old coming down to teach a bunch of mean eigth graders a lesson. There'd be something satisfying about it, but also something silly.

"I don't think so," Cole replied. Most of the paint was gone by now.

"*Now* what did they do?" a voice asked. Cole looked up to see Riley and some of her friends.

Jason was a little surprised by their presence; Cole hadn't mentioned Riley to him. He hadn't thought there was a need to.

Just then, a posse of snickering boys came by, Dennis in front of them.

One of the boys gestured at Riley and her friends.

"Are these your new bodyguards?" he asked.

"Or are they your personal volleyball coaches?" Dennis chimed in.

"You're the one who's going to need a body-guard," Riley shot back. "You're building up some really bad karma, and it's all going to come back at you soon."

"Is that a threat?" the boy asked.

"No," Riley said with a smile, "it's a promise."

Some of the guys laughed — not at Riley, but with her. Cole was really glad she was on his side.

The boys passed, and Riley and her friends went on their way.

Jason shot Cole a questioning look. "Who was *that?*"

"Just a friend."

"Just a friend," Jason mimicked. He was really enjoying watching Cole squirm under the attention of a girl.

"Stop it!"

"Stop it!"

Cole took a wad of wet paper towels and threw it at Jason. Jason threw it back at him. Things might have escalated if Ms. Keller hadn't walked into the halls just then, looking sternly at Cole, sizing up his behavior.

"She's out to get you," Jason whispered as she passed.

She's not the only one, Cole answered to himself.

*　*　*

John Heginbotham closed in as soon as Jason had left. Cole was beginning to hear his footsteps even when he wasn't there. They haunted his every move. They would not go away.

That afternoon, there was an all-school assembly. A local author was coming to read from his new book and answer students' questions about being a writer. Cole went to the auditorium with his English class, Ms. Grant leading the way.

The stage of the auditorium was decorated with the author's book covers. Cole had read a few of the books and liked them a lot. He was surprised when the author came on stage; he was much younger than Cole had pictured. Cole had figured anyone who had written ten books had to be at least sixty years old. But this writer looked not much older than Cole's mom.

The principal welcomed the author to the school and then Ms. Larkin gave him a proper introduction, talking about his books and how often they'd been taken out of the library over the years. When she was finished, she sat down next to the principal on the stage. The author stood up, made a few jokes, and then began to read from one of his books.

Cole noticed how the author's voice changed when he was reading out loud, how he started to become one of the characters. He wasn't just reading the story, he was *telling* the story. Even though he was describing castles and dragons and other imaginary things, Cole believed for a moment that they were real. The author could use words to conjure up a whole world.

Cole was lost for a moment in this world . . . then a very familiar sound sent him crashing back to reality.

The footsteps.

John Heginbotham was coming out on the stage, his face warped into an evil grin. He looked out at the audience, searching for Cole, trying to get his attention. Cole sunk low in his seat. It was possible the hanged man couldn't see him. It was possible he would just move on.

The author continued to read, his words picking up pitch, carrying the characters through fields and caverns. The kids listened, enraptured, quieter than in any assembly Cole could remember. Some of them closed their eyes to hear the words better. None of them saw the dead man walking across the stage. None of them but Cole.

Stay calm. I must stay calm.

Heginbotham was behind the principal's chair now, still searching the crowd with his blood-tinged eyes. Cole held his breath, as if that could somehow make him invisible. He looked to his left, where Ms. Grant was sitting two chairs away. She, too, was lost in the author's words. There wasn't a thing she could do to help.

Cole looked back to the stage. The hanged man was now behind Ms. Larkin, her small, birdlike frame dwarfed by his monstrous standing height. She had no idea, *no idea whatsoever*, that a dead man was pressing against her back. Cole could see a shudder of cold pass through her. But still she looked at the visiting author, delighting in his reading. She would not turn and see the dead man's hands approaching.

Cole sat up now. Heginbotham was moving his pale fingers around Ms. Larkin's unaware throat. Then, much to Cole's relief, he pulled back.

Relief, however, soon turned to horror.

Heginbotham reached up to the noose around his neck. As Cole watched, shocked, Heginbotham loosened the rope and pulled it over his face. Then he took the deadly noose and held it over Ms. Larkin's head.

No . . .

With deliberate steadiness, the hanged man put the noose around the librarian's neck. She didn't struggle. She didn't scream. She didn't know what was happening. Heginbotham began to tighten the circle. The rope began to grip her neck.

Tighter . . . and tighter . . .

Ms. Larkin started to gasp.

Cole shot up from his chair, screaming.

"NO!"

ELEVEN

The author stopped reading. A sea of faces turned toward Cole. Ms. Larkin moved her hand to her throat. She didn't know why she had just felt like she was choking. There wasn't any rope there. There wasn't any dead man behind her. They were gone.

Cole hadn't realized what he was doing. He had crashed the whole assembly with his scream.

Now there was nothing but realization for Cole. He took in the looks on everyone's faces. The author was confused. The principal was enraged. The kids around him were startled. Other kids were beginning to whisper and jeer. They were all talking about him. He had broken the spell. This assembly was now like any other assembly — a chance for rumors and jokes to spread. He might have saved Ms. Larkin's life. But there was no way for any of them to know that.

He was still standing. He couldn't sit back down. And he couldn't stay either.

So he bolted. He pushed past the kid on his left, past Ms. Grant sitting on the aisle. As the whole school watched, he jerked open the auditorium door and fled into the hallway. He could hear the taunts of the older boys in the back row — "There goes the spaz!" "He really *is* a freak" — and he could imagine the shock on Jason's and Riley's faces when they realized he wasn't really worth their friendship.

He had no idea where to go. He heard footsteps behind him and tried to ignore them. It wasn't the death shuffle of the hanged man, though. It was Ms. Grant, looking both bewildered and concerned.

Cole let her catch up to him. There was no use in running away.

Cole figured she would yell at him for ruining the assembly, but instead she asked, "Cole, are you okay?"

He looked at her and didn't know how to answer. If he told her he wasn't okay, she'd want to know why. There was no way to explain it to her.

"What happened back there?" Ms. Grant continued. "I saw you Cole. You were seeing something.

And then you just screamed. Like you were waking up from a nightmare. Was that it?"

I can't explain. Please don't ask me to explain.

Ms. Grant leaned over and looked him straight in the eye.

"I want to help you, Cole. You're going to get into big trouble for this. You have no idea how often I've fought for you. But things like this don't make it easy."

So give up. Stop fighting for me. I don't deserve it. I'm not going to change.

"Cole, are you listening to me?"

It's always going to be the same.

Maybe Cole's expression gave Ms. Grant all the answers she needed, because she took another look at him and stopped asking questions.

"Don't worry," she said. "It will be all right."

She sounded like she was trying to convince both of them it was true.

A minute later, the principal found them. He didn't have any kind words or gentle questions. He was furious — and all of his anger was directed at Cole. He told Cole he was a disgrace to the school, and that he had embarrassed both himself and all of his fellow students in front of a distinguished guest. Dismissing Ms. Grant back to her students in the auditorium, he personally escorted Cole down to the office and called Cole's mom to come pick him up. Cole couldn't hear his mom's end of the conversation, but he knew it was bad.

Once he was assured that Cole's mom would pick him up immediately, the principal stormed back out of the office to conclude the assembly. Cole was left alone with the two office secretaries, who he always thought of as Good and Evil. Good shot him sympathetic looks and told him he could go get his books from his locker before his mom arrived. Evil glared at him like he'd just committed a murder; she had this reaction to every student transgression, whether it was showing up late for class or innocently dropping off a permission slip in the wrong box.

Since he knew it would take at least ten minutes for Lynn to get to the school to pick him up, Cole decided to take Good up on her offer and head to his locker. It was strange to have the school so deserted — with the students and teachers in the assembly, most of the people around were dead. Cole walked by the family of former slaves dangling from their nooses, and stumbled past the janitor's closet with the sound of restless sweeping coming from inside. He got to his locker, still smeared with the red blur of former insults. He tried to think of the good things about the school, the reasons he wanted to keep coming here. His friends. The teachers he liked. The feeling that he belonged.

But that feeling was starting to fade, as if it had never really existed.

Do I really belong here? Is there anywhere I really belong?

He put his books in his backpack and slammed his locker shut.

The footsteps began again.

He could see John Heginbotham coming this time, trudging in his death step down the halls. Cole wondered if this was the way he was led in the last minutes of his life. Did he shout his innocence to this hallway? Did anyone listen?

And what if they were right not to listen? What if he really *was* guilty?

Cole shuddered — this time not from the cold, but from the grim possibility that he was being haunted by someone who had been guilty as charged. Someone who could never be proved innocent . . . because he wasn't.

"What do you want, then?" Cole shouted. He didn't care who heard, as long as he got through to the hanged man. "Why are you trying to scare me? To get my attention? To make me lie for you and say you didn't do it? WHY?"

Could Heginbotham even hear him? Was there a

real person left inside the ravaged shell of a hanged body? What if the dead man no longer knew why he wandered? What if he was demented, unstable, out for revenge against a wrong he couldn't even remember?

He said nothing. He opened his mouth, but said nothing. His eyes, barely alive, bore into Cole, but they couldn't convey any message. He gestured down to his feet, pointed to the floor. Cole had no idea what he meant.

Cole could hear a rush of voices in the distance. The assembly was over; soon the halls would be full. Cole didn't want to be caught here — not by the bullies, not even by his friends. He didn't want to have to explain anything to anyone. He wanted to retreat back into the world where it was only him and his problems. It seemed like the only place to go. It seemed like there wasn't any choice.

His mom was waiting for him in the office. She must have sped to get here. Evil was staring her down with a disapproving glance; Lynn Sear mirrored her look back at her, just as disapproving. When she saw Cole, the expression didn't really change.

"Do you have your things?" she asked flatly.

Cole nodded.

" 'Bye now," the Good secretary chirped.

Cole followed his mother all the way to the car. It wasn't until they were both buckled up in the front seat that she talked.

"I am so angry at you right now that I'm afraid of what will come out of my mouth," she said. "I need to calm down and get back to work as soon as humanly possible. You need to go home, do all of your homework, and prepare to explain to me why you would get on your feet and scream in the middle of a school assembly. I know you, Cole, and I know you wouldn't do something like that without a reason. But right now I'm not ready to hear that reason. Do you understand?"

"Yes."

They rode in silence until they got to the house. Lynn was already a little calmer.

"I'll see you tonight, okay?" she said.

"Yes."

"And you know I love you no matter what, right?"

"Right."

"I just want you to tell me the truth."

"I will."

"Okay. I have to get back."

"I love you, too."

Lynn pulled the car back onto the street so fast that Cole was afraid she'd get into an accident. He knew she wasn't rushing away from him, but back to the place he'd taken her from. He hoped she wasn't in as much trouble as he was.

That night, she was barely on time for dinner. Over a reheated pan of lasagna, he told her what had happened at the assembly, and why he'd screamed out. He told her about John Heginbotham, and how he'd been haunting the school.

"I don't believe it," Lynn said when Cole was through. "I mean, I believe *you,* but I don't believe *it.* Does that make any sense?"

Cole nodded.

"What are we going to do?" Lynn asked.

Cole wanted to ask her the same question.

Neither of them had the answer.

That night, they were both miserable. For the same reasons, and for different ones, too.

TWELVE

Cole's mom was gone when he woke up the next morning. This had never happened before. She left a note on the kitchen table, saying she had gotten up really early and realized there were things she could do at the office before Mr. Richardson came in. She hadn't wanted to wake Cole to say good-bye. She told him in her note to have a good day. He wondered how that would be possible.

He dreaded going to school. He was exhausted — his eyes could barely open and his throat was always dry. And still he had every intention of going to school. He put on his school clothes. He had breakfast and made his lunch. He packed his homework in his bag. He made sure he was out of the house on time, and that the door was double-locked behind him.

It was only when he was a block away from school that his mind started to get other ideas. He saw Dennis and a group of bullies milling around the front door, looking around. Were they waiting for him? Was there any way to avoid them for a whole day? He also saw Jason talking to some of his other friends. Cole wondered if they were talking about him, too. Was Jason defending him? Did it annoy Jason to have to defend Cole all the time? Would he get tired of it — and stop?

He thought of Ms. Grant's confused concern. He pictured the way Ms. Larkin would act the next time she saw him — would she even have a hint of why he'd done what he'd done, or would she merely see him as the disturbed kid who wrecked the assembly?

Cole didn't plan on finding out. Not today.

John Heginbotham would be waiting for him in school. John Heginbotham and all the other dead people. Dead adults. Dead kids. Each with his or her own story and desire. Each with his or her own bitterness or denial. Each wanting something from Cole. Pulling him this way and that. Pulling him apart.

Cole didn't exactly decide to cut school; he just

found himself walking the other way. Part of him was leading, and part of him couldn't believe what he was doing. No matter how bad things got, he'd never skipped out like this before. He'd pretended he was sick and stayed up under his mom's watch — but he'd never taken off without her permission. He didn't want to think about her now, or how she'd react. Right now, all he wanted to do was get away.

He headed back to the public library. He had to find more there. He had to find the truth about the hanged man. There was no other way to get rid of him.

So Cole returned to the haunted shelves, the trespassed corridors, and the lonely archives of words both living and dead. He walked through the whispers of the reading room and the carpeted quiet of the darker corners.

"Can I help you?" a librarian asked. Cole could tell from her tone that her real question was *Why aren't you in school?*

"I'm researching a report," he said, then added, "I'm home-schooled. My mom is in the fiction section."

The librarian looked relieved. Cole remembered the articles he'd ordered the last time he was here. The librarian checked and came back saying they'd been delayed. Maybe another week or so . . .

Cole tried to hide his disappointment. He went to the periodical room to see if there were any newspapers from 1814; there were, but there wasn't any index, and the issues were sporadic at best. Cole loaded the scratched-and-blurry microfilm into its machine and whirred through the days, trying to spy Heginbotham's name amidst the cattle sales, shipping news, and dead politics. He found an account of Heginbotham's arrest, but none of the trial. Of the arrest, it was written:

Heginbotham was taken from his home on Spring Street and charged with treason. He protested his innocence as friends looked on from the street. He was taken to Magistrate Pim of the Philadelphia court, who read the charges and asked for a plea.

Heginbotham asked to consult with a lawyer, and the arraignment was postponed until tomorrow. It is charged that Heginbotham colluded with the British and has acted as a spy. If convicted, the maximum punishment is death.

There were no newspapers remaining from the month of December, when Heginbotham had been hanged. There was, however, one short article from May, which said he was being kept in a cell in the lowest level of the jail. Curious, Cole went to the librarian and together they searched out a map of the old building. (Cole was careful not to let the librarian know it was also his school.)

It was strange for Cole to see the familiar hallways rearranged into cells and gallows. Sure enough, the executions took place in what was now the gym. The prisoners who were going to be killed were kept below the main level, what was now known as the sub-basement. Nobody but the janitors went down there anymore.

Cole flipped ahead to another map of the building, still before it became his school. The cells were still in the basement, but there was a new room there, labeled ARCHIVES. Cole wondered what the archives held.

Cole made copies of the map and printed out a few of the articles from the microfilm. Then he headed to the periodical computer, just to make sure he didn't miss anything. He typed in John Heginbotham's name and found the same articles he'd found before, most of them written by Professor Rohlfing. Then he typed in Professor Rohlfing's name, just in case there was something he was missing.

More than a few articles came up. Most of them were scholarly articles about historical figures.

But a few of the articles weren't *by* David Rohlfing. They were *about* David Rohlfing.

And they were dated four years ago. About the time the other articles ended.

Cole clicked and double-clicked. He ran to the bound-up tabloids and the more recent microfilm.

Suddenly, it was all making sense. Cole knew why Professor Rohlfing had stopped writing. He knew why Professor Rohlfing's house appeared the way it did.

He also knew what he'd have to do the next time he went there.

It wouldn't be easy . . . but it had to be done.

Cole had to see for himself.

THIRTEEN

Nobody was home at Professor Rohlfing's house that afternoon — or at least nobody answered the door. Cole rang the bell again and again, but it was no use. There was no way for him to get in.

School wasn't over yet, but there was no reason to go there now. Cole figured that since his mom was at work and his neighbors didn't care, it would be safe for him to sneak home. He would have some time to prepare his lies and figure out what he'd do about returning to school the next day. He was surprised at how easy it had been to cut; he'd expected a truancy officer to grab him and pull him back to class. But no such officer existed. Cole was a free kid.

He was so lost in thought that he didn't see his mom's car on the street when he walked up to the apartment. He didn't notice that the door was only single-locked. He didn't see what was coming until it was right in front of his face — his mom on a chair in the living room, looking small and lost . . . and wondering why on earth he had just come through the door.

"Why aren't you at school?" she asked.

"Why aren't you at work?" he asked back, stalling for time.

"Because I was fired, Cole. Or I quit. I still can't tell which."

This was the worst possible news.

Lynn was crying now. Cole walked over to her and put his hand on her shoulder.

"What do you mean?" he whispered.

"I mean, it's over. It's been a long time coming. Yesterday, when I had to go to your school, Mr. Richardson told me I couldn't leave the office. He said I was needed there, and that I couldn't let my personal problems *interfere* with the workplace. I didn't say a thing to him. I just got my keys and left. He screamed out at me to not bother coming back. But I came back. I told him I would get in early today to make up for the twenty-five minutes I'd missed — as if I wasn't going to stay the usual three hours late anyway.

"So I get in early, do some things, and as soon as he hits the office, he's yelling at me. Saying I'm lazy. Saying I'm not doing a good job. *Maybe this isn't working out,* he says. And I know he's expecting that I'll beg for my job. He knows my situation. He knows how much we need the money. But now that he's called me on it, I know that I have to leave.

"So I tell him it isn't working out for me, either. And I could have just left it at that, but my mouth got the best of me. I'm telling him that I'm sick of being overworked and underappreciated. I'm telling him that I wasn't hired to be his personal assistant — I was hired to keep his books and numbers in order. I'm telling him it's indecent to make someone feel guilty for having to bail out her son from school. It's wrong the way he hovers over me whenever my phone rings, checking to see if it's a personal call. I tell him I need the money, but I don't need it that bad. I tell him I quit. He tells me I'm already fired. And I tell him, no, I *quit.*"

She seemed proud while she was telling this story, but when she finished, the sadness and the fear came back to her face.

Cole pulled away a little, his face too full of sadness and fear. "It's my fault, isn't it?"

Lynn shook her head. "What do you mean?"

Cole had to say it all now. He had to get it out of his head. "If you didn't have to come and get me at school . . . if I wasn't getting into trouble all the time . . . you wouldn't have been fired —"

"I *quit*, Cole."

"Well, you wouldn't have had to quit. We wouldn't be out of money."

Lynn reached over and took Cole's face in her hands, raising his head so his eyes matched hers. "Look at my face, Cole," she said. "This is *not your fault*. It's not *my* fault. It's something that just happened. Mr. Richardson wasn't a very nice guy. He paid me okay, but he wasn't a good boss. I haven't been happy at work for a very long time. You know that, don't you?"

Cole nodded.

"If it wasn't your school conference or having to pick you up, it would have been something else. With people like Mr. Richardson, there's always something else. I'll be able to find another job. Moira's always asking me to help her at the shop more than I already do, so maybe I'll do that for a little while, hang out with the antiques. And something else will come along. I swear, in the end this could be the best thing that ever happened to me."

Cole wanted to believe this. But his head came back to the same thought — it was all his fault. Sure, his mom might have quit the job eventually, when she'd found a better job. But the bottom line was that if she hadn't had to come pick him up at school yesterday, she'd still be at the office right now.

"So why aren't you in school?"

Cole's mom was looking straight into his eyes, and all at once all the lies and stories fell from his head.

"I didn't go to school," he said, looking away.

"You *what?*"

"I didn't go to school. I couldn't."

"You *couldn't?*"

"These guys were waiting for me outside. And the dead people were inside. I just couldn't."

Lynn Sear stood up, as if she needed to be standing to get her full message across.

"Cole, you can't just cut school when you don't want to deal with things. God knows there were days when I didn't want to face Mr. Richardson or any of the things that were waiting for me at work. But I *went.* I sucked it up and I went."

"But Mom —"

"Not buts, Cole. No excuses." She paused and looked at her purse; Cole knew that even though she'd stopped smoking, she was still instinctively looking around for a cigarette. "I can't believe this. I really can't. You can't do this to me, Cole. You can't do this to yourself. I don't mind losing the job. Really, I don't, when I look at it. But I *do* mind you doing something like this. I am trying so hard, Cole. And you're trying. We've been surviving, haven't we? You can't throw that away. You go to a very good school. One of the best in the city. I've used up most of our savings to put you through. And don't think for a second that I mind doing that. But you have to hold up your end of the bargain. You have to do your best. You can't get into trouble. And I know it's one thing when the dead people are around. I know that's hard. But what you did today doesn't really have anything to do with them, does it? You can't just run away from things."

Not like your father. Not like Detective Brown's brother, who was never seen again.

Cole saw the anger in his mother's eyes, and also the love. He saw how torn she was, and he felt awful for tearing her. He wished he could erase the day and start all over again. He wished he could say a lie and find out it had become the truth.

But there was no way to turn back the clock, or alter reality. He'd disappointed her right when she needed him the most. That was the inescapable truth.

"I need to think, Cole," Lynn said now, sitting back down in her chair, putting her face in her hands. Her voice was fragile, worn thin. "There are so many things I need to think about. I need to be able to not worry about you. I need to know that you're doing the right thing. I don't have the energy, Cole, not for everything at once. I need to save it up to get us to the next step. Do you hear me?"

"Yes," Cole said, walking over and putting his hand again on her back. He remembered the times she used to come home all tense, and he would give her backrubs, and she would say he'd made everything better. He didn't even try that now — he knew he couldn't make everything better. He'd just have to work on his part of it. He would have to stay out of trouble.

"I'm sorry, Mom," he whispered.

"So am I, hon. So am I."

He went to his room to do his homework, even though he wasn't sure what the assignments were. His mom started to call all of her friends to tell them what had happened with Mr. Richardson; as she did, her indignation grew, and she started to come back to life. Her strength was returning, but Cole knew from experience that it was a very vulnerable strength. All it took was one thing to go wrong and everything else would topple down.

It would be up to Cole to avoid being that one thing.

FOURTEEN

The next morning, Cole's mom wrote him a note saying he'd been home sick from school.

"I'm not going to let you get kicked out because of this," she said, looking extremely vexed as she wrote the excuse on her stationery. "I've worked too hard for you to go to that school. But let me tell you — if you ever, *ever* cut school again, I will march down there and pull you out myself. Am I understood?"

Cole nodded. He felt horrible about everything that had happened. He tried to imagine what his mom would do once he left the house. He was used to their morning routine — getting ready for school and for work, heading out the door at about the same time, knowing the house would be empty until they came home again. But now it was only Cole leaving for the day; all through school he would picture his mom at home, pacing around, wondering what to do next.

Cole knew it wasn't his fault that she'd been fired, but he still *felt* like it was his fault.

He couldn't tell her this. It would only make her feel worse.

So he tried to pretend it was just another morning. When he kissed her good-bye for the day, he pretended that she was already dressed for work. He pretended she was happy, and that the day would be a good one for both of them.

But of course it wasn't going to be a good one. There wasn't a note in the world that would prevent Cole from getting all kinds of attention he didn't want. As he walked to school, he remembered the humiliation of the assembly — the moment everyone was looking at him, not knowing why he'd screamed. *Spaz. Freak. Loser.* If the taunts had been bad before, they'd be horrible now.

As he handed in his mother's note at the principal's office, Evil gave him a knowing, mean look. *I know why you were really out yesterday,* it seemed to say. *You're a coward. A crazy person. You don't fit in here at all.* Even Good seemed to strain a little at her smile; Cole could tell from the effort it took her that he was in for a very long day.

John Heginbotham was waiting for him outside the office, his expression more desperate and deranged than ever. He pounded his feet with fervor. Then, to Cole's bewilderment, he crawled down and started to scratch at the floor. His inarticulate cry was full of fear and anger.

Cole kept his distance. He tried to walk around the hanged man. Then he felt a hand grab hard on his backpack.

He turned to find one of the older guys from the library, wearing an insult-ready expression.

"Hey, look who's back," the boy said to some of his friends. "Do you think he wants to scream for us again?"

"EEEK! HELP ME!" the other boys chimed in, mimicking a little girl's cry.

The boy wouldn't let go of Cole's backpack. The harder Cole pulled, the harder the kid pulled back. Cole thought of abandoning his pack all together, and just running off.

He yanked. Hard. This time the boy let go, and Cole went stumbling to the floor, a few feet from where Heginbotham scratched and wailed. The hall was filled with laughter. Not just the kids who'd been teasing Cole, but other kids who were walking by. Cole was the main attraction — the star freak.

He shouldn't have looked at the dead man. Because of course someone shouted, "Hey, what are you looking at? You like my shoes or something?" and another round of smirking and guffawing followed. It wasn't even that funny; the kids were just getting excited about getting him down. That was the sickest part of it.

"Leave him alone!"

It was Riley, pushing into the fray with some of her friends, making it even worse.

"Hey, man, it's your girlfriend!"

"Save him! Save him!"

"EEEEK!"

Cole was back on his feet now. He had his backpack. Riley was coming over and the boys were hooting. It was like being under a spotlight. Total pressure.

"Are you okay?" she asked *in front of everybody else*. Like he was a baby who'd fallen off a swing. Cole knew he was probably reading it the wrong way — he knew he was too caught up in the humiliation of the moment — but he couldn't help snapping at her — he couldn't help saying, "Leave me alone!" and pulling away — which only made the boys start mimicking *"Leave me alone! Leave me alone!"* Riley's expression changed from concern to a complicated, confused hurt. Cole was sorry — he really was. But how could he explain? How could he tell her that the hanged man writhing at her feet was going to follow him through school for the rest of the day? How could he tell her that there were other dead people pressuring him, appearing to him, ruining his life? How could he tell her that the reason he snapped at her wasn't just because everyone was looking at him and judging him and finding him insane — it was also because his mom had lost her job and he had lost his calm and the day had been totally lost since the moment he had first woken up, the taint of a nightmare still on his mind. He couldn't say any of this — he couldn't even say "sorry" — because the bell was ringing and the show was over and he was letting everyone walk away. Because if he was the one to run away, it wouldn't turn the spotlight off. It would only make it follow.

Later in the morning, Cole went to the nurse's office to avoid gym. She took one look at him and didn't ask any questions. She let him lie down in one of the cots and wrestle with his thoughts. Two cots over, a girl had stretched herself out, absolutely still. Cole had seen her before; he knew she'd died fifteen years ago. She'd had an attack while she was at school. The nurse was out that day and the substitute didn't realize how serious it was. The girl's parents were called, but by the time they came, it was too late. They didn't make it to the hospital on time. So now the girl stared at the ceiling from a white, stripped-down bed. Although Cole had noticed her, she had never noticed Cole. She was no longer looking for anyone.

Cole tried not to consider what Riley would think when he didn't show up at gym. He tried not to wonder how the bullies would react. For the second question, Cole would get an answer much sooner than he wanted. When he stepped out of the nurse's office a minute or two before the period was over, Dennis was there, waiting for him.

"You're making Dennis mad," the kid said, laying into Cole immediately. "You think you can get away from Dennis, but you can't. Dennis found you, spaz. And Dennis is just starting to have fun."

The nurse's office was in a corner of the school; the hallway was deserted before the bell rang.

Cole felt defenseless.

Dennis closed in. He raised his fist and threw a punch, stopping a few inches from Cole's face.

"What, no scream?" Dennis asked. "I wanted to hear you scream again."

Why are you doing this? Cole thought. *Why can't you leave me alone? What have I ever done to you?*

Dennis was a little thrown off by Cole's silence.

"Believe me," he said, "Dennis can make you scream. Isn't that right?"

When Cole didn't answer, he yelled it again: "ISN'T THAT RIGHT?"

"Yes," Cole whispered.

Let me go. I am holding back, but I won't hold back much longer.

Dennis studied Cole for a moment, then seemed pleased. He figured he's scared Cole to a satisfactory level.

"See you later, then," he said with a self-important snarl. "You better be ready to scream again, freak."

As soon as Dennis turned a corner, Cole breathed normally again.

Please let me make it through this day.

Cole tried to remain calm in Ms. Grant's class, even though John Heginbotham was at the front of the room again, howling and flailing with choked rage. After class, Ms. Grant asked him if everything was okay. This time he didn't snap at the question, and instead fell back once more on pretending.

"Things are fine," he said, shuffling his feet.

Ms. Grant didn't look like she believed him.

Cole's best friend Jason also didn't look like he believed him when Cole said at lunch that he'd been out sick yesterday.

"Yeah, right," Jason said. "You probably milked the sympathy points with your mom and got to watch game shows all day. I totally approve of that."

Cole just smiled, letting Jason think what he wanted to think. Cole was psyched to have someone's approval, even for the wrong reasons.

Things with Jason were going fine until John Heginbotham came clamoring into the cafeteria. He spotted Cole right away and began to finger his noose. He looked at all the other kids innocently eating their lunches. He was targeting them. Then his gaze fell on Jason, sitting right across from Cole. The dead man knew how to get to Cole. And Cole knew he had to get away before anything awful happened.

"I gotta go," he said to Jason, even though Jason was in the middle of a sentence. He already knew what Jason's next sentence would be — *Are you okay?* — so he gathered his tray and headed out before he'd have to answer.

I just have to ride the rest of the school day out, Cole thought.

Then he would go to Professor Rohlfing's house . . . and he wouldn't leave until the man let him in.

FIFTEEN

Professor Rohlfing didn't answer the first ring of the doorbell. Or the second. Or the fifth.

He answered on the thirteenth ring.

He didn't look at all pleased when he came to the door. He looked extremely put out. And his expression didn't change when he saw it was Cole. There'd be no kindness for Cole here.

"What do you want?" the professor asked, his voice verging on hostile. "It is not a good time."

"I only have a few questions —" Cole began.

"Isn't your report due already?" Rohlfing interrupted. "Shouldn't you be writing it yourself instead of asking me to do all the work? I'm telling you — I am through with writing, I am through with Heginbotham, I am through with investigating, and right now, I'm afraid, I must be through with you. I do not appreciate you showing up at my doorstep like this, no matter how scholarly your intentions. My wife isn't feeling well, and I must go tend to her. So if you'll excuse me, I must go."

Cole remembered the horrible truth of what he'd read about Rohlfing in the library. He tried to think of a way to get himself inside. He thought maybe he could help . . . but there was no way to tell Rohlfing this directly. There had to be some other way. . . .

"Please," Cole said, stalling for time. Then he thought of something. It helped that it was the truth.

"There's nobody else who can help me," he said. "My dad is gone and my mother just lost her job. My teachers can't help, because they don't know things like you do. You're the only person. Please."

Suddenly the professor wasn't seeing him as one of his students, or as a nuisance at the door. No, he was seeing him as he really was — an eleven-year-old boy who needed help.

"Come in," the professor said reluctantly, opening the door. "Just please be quiet. My wife is in her room."

They sat again in the parlor. Cole could still hear a slight rocking noise from upstairs.

"Why didn't anyone believe John Heginbotham

when he said he was innocent?" Cole asked. *Why had everyone ganged up against him? Why hadn't his friends stood by him?*

"You have to understand that there was a war going on," the professor explained. "When the war began, we were totally unprepared to beat the British. Our army was supposed to have 36,700 men — but fewer than ten thousand had been raised. The U.S. had sixteen frigates and sloops of war. The British Navy had over six hundred vessels. We thought we'd be okay since the British were also fighting the French at the time, and most of their army was being used there. But when Napoleon was defeated in 1814, thousands of veteran British troops were available for service in America. Suddenly we weren't on the attack anymore — we had to defend our country. In August of 1814 they took D.C. and burned most of the government buildings down. When Heginbotham was hanged, they were moving on towards Baltimore. Luckily, they were turned back, but the damage was done. Even the people who had been against the war were for it by now. And they had no sympathy for a spy — especially one they thought had been their friend.

"It was actually one of Heginbotham's closer friends who'd testified against him, and had said he'd seen Heginbotham with British agents. Colonel

Steven Anderson of the American Army — he wasn't a colonel back then, but he became one later, in the Jackson administration. If Anderson hadn't informed the authorities, I don't know if Heginbotham would have ever been accused and tried. I have one of Anderson's letters, if you'd like to see it."

Cole said he would love to see it.

"Now where is it, then?" the professor asked. "Oh yes, the basement. This might take a few minutes. I'll be back. The kitchen is over there if you need some water."

This was the moment Cole had been waiting for. He knew he was taking a risk, but he had to do it. As he heard Rohlfing's footsteps go to the cellar, Cole jumped out of his chair and headed to the second floor.

Upstairs the house was dusty, unkempt. Not meant for visitors.

Cole steered clear of the master bedroom. He could hear Mrs. Rohlfing inside, coughing.

He was looking for another room. The room above the parlor. The room that the rocking sound had come from.

Quietly, he creeped down the hall, past the bathroom, past a guest room. Then there was a closed door with a small glint of light coming from underneath.

This was it.

Cole knocked and a surprised voice told him to come in.

It was a teenage girl's room, and inside was a teenage girl. Her hair was dyed raven black. Her pale face was covered by dozen of tiny cuts, each caused by a splinter of broken glass. She was sitting in a rocking chair that faced the door.

"Come in," she said again, composed now. "I've been waiting for you, even though I didn't know it would be you. You can see me, can't you?"

Cole closed the door behind him and nodded.

"Do you know my parents?" the girl asked.

"I know your father."

"You're way too young to be one of his students."

"He's helping me on a project."

The girl nodded. "He's good at that. There was this one time I had to do a leaf project for my science class. I swear, my teacher was a psycho — he wanted us to get fifty different kinds of leaves from different trees around here. And then we had to identify them all! It nearly drove me crazy. But Dad kept me going. He drove me around — the night before the project was due, I only had forty-nine leaves, so we wandered around the city until we found this little maple tree in someone's backyard. We were both so excited — you would've thought we'd found a tree that grew money. We ran back home, pasted it into the report, and then got a few hours of sleep before I had to go to school the next day. I got an A on the project. I remember that."

She paused in her memory, smiling as she relived it in echo. Then her smile faded. She was drawn to the present.

"What happened?" Cole asked, even though he already knew some of the answer from the newspaper articles.

"Oh, it started off as a normal fight," the girl began. "I think the leaf project was the last A I ever got — and that was in eighth grade. Now I was a senior and I didn't care about school. Mom and Dad were always on my case, bugging me about college. And I just closed them out. My SAT scores were really lame, and my applications were all late. All I wanted to do was spend time with my friends. I wanted to have fun. I didn't care that I had to take the SATs over again. There was this party I wanted to go to the night before. Mom and Dad said I couldn't go. I said some really awful things to them — called them names, said I was free to do what I wanted to do — the worst. They took away my car keys and told me I was grounded.

"Once they did that, there was no way I was going to miss that party. So I snuck out. Mom was asleep and Dad was working. I walked right past his door, but he didn't hear me. He was too caught up in writing history.

"My friend Alex picked me up. It wasn't until I was in the car that I realized how drunk he was. Mom and Dad had told me never, ever to get into a car with a drunk driver. I knew that. But I chose to stay in the car anyway. I figured Alex wasn't that out of it, and the party wasn't far."

Cole was feeling colder and colder as the girl talked. Now it was she who shuddered, remembering the night of her death.

"He just lost control," she said quietly. "One moment we were in the right lane. The next moment we were in the left lane and there were trucks and cars coming at us. We didn't have a chance. I was in the front seat, but I wasn't wearing my seat belt. Another thing my parents would never have let me get away with.

"Mom's been out of her head ever since. Dad's taken care of her — it's like his full-time job. They got an unlisted phone number and stopped seeing their friends. Maybe if I had brothers or sisters, it would be different. But it's just the two of them."

"And they feel guilty?" Cole asked.

The girl nodded. "Yes. They think it's their fault. They think if only they hadn't taken my keys, I would have been the one driving, and the accident would never have happened. None of us would have died. Or if they hadn't grounded me, then maybe I wouldn't have gotten into the car with Alex. Who knows? It's just so wrong — it wasn't their fault at all. I knew what I was doing. It was my choice. And it was a stupid choice. Now Mom's stopped doing anything, and Dad only works when he has to. It's like he thinks he would've heard me sneak out if he hadn't been working. So now he doesn't work. But I'm not going to be sneaking back in."

Cole remembered other people he had helped, other people who had needed to talk to people who were still alive.

"Talk to them," he told Professor Rohlfing's daughter. "Talk to them when they're sleeping lightly. Tell them what you have to say."

"It's hard for me to move."

"You have to make yourself get there."

"Can't *you* tell them?"

Cole shook his head. "They won't believe me." *And once living people start to know I can talk to the dead, life as I know it would be over. I'd really be the star freak then.*

The girl seemed satisfied with Cole's answer.

"I'll try," she said.

Just then, Professor Rohlfing's voice interrupted from downstairs. He was calling for Cole, no doubt wondering where he'd gone.

"I better go," Cole said.

"Thank you," the girl whispered.

Cole didn't turn back as he silently shut the door and hurried downstairs. He dodged into the kitchen, then came back to the parlor.

"I was going to get some water like you told me to," he told the professor, "but I couldn't find a glass."

Rohlfing looked at him suspiciously for a moment, then put his papers down and retrieved a glass of water for Cole from the kitchen.

"Colonel Anderson is very explicit in his letters about the evidence against Heginbotham," the professor explained once he settled into his chair. "Heginbotham had access to military plans. He was seen copying them, although he would argue that he was copying them for his own use, to help him remember the strategies. He was seen with men later known to be British agents. The British, in turn, were surprisingly knowledgeable when they attacked the District of Columbia.

"It seems like an open-shut case. But things rarely are. Anderson himself profited from Heginbotham's trial — his rank increased steadily after he turned his friend in — and Anderson himself had access to the same things Heginbotham did. Yes, Heginbotham was seen with British agents. But these same British agents were part of Philadelphia, and had private conversations with just about anyone who was anyone in this town, mostly about politics and fashion — neither of which are treason to discuss. Heginbotham admitted to conversing with them, but said they'd talked about whether or not America was wise to declare war — *not* about military plans. Anderson insisted that he overheard a conversation that mentioned much more than that — but we only have Anderson's word for it."

Cole started to piece together what Professor Rohlfing was saying. "So if Anderson was lying, then Heginbotham might have been innocent?" he asked.

The professor nodded. "Yes. But that's a big *if* and an even bigger *might*. In order to draw a conclusion like that, you need proof."

"And you can't find any?"

"No. Anderson's letters exist — I have copies here — but they are pretty consistent in recalling events. He even says that Heginbotham stopped claiming his innocence on the day he died; he just went silently to the gallows. If Anderson's lying, he's very good at sticking to the lie. As I told you, the

London archives are no help, since the pertinent papers presumably were destroyed in a fire. And I've checked the court archives here, but they're a complete mess."

"The court archives?" Cole asked. "Where are those?"

"Why, in the basement of your school," Professor Rohlfing replied.

Cole remembered the maps of what was now the sub-basement. *Archives.*

"I'm sure students aren't allowed there," the professor continued. "There's no reason you'd know about it. I think the only people who have access are the city archivist and your school librarian."

Ms. Larkin . . .

It was all starting to come together for Cole. John Heginbotham hadn't just been making random threats. He had been pointing Cole in a direction.

Pointing to the ground and scratching at the ground — *go down to the sub-basement.*

Putting the noose around Ms. Larkin's neck — *she's the one who will let you go there.*

Lunging at Cole so he would grab Professor Rohlfing's book — *Professor Rohlfing is the only one who can clear his name in the history books. If only Professor Rohlfing starts to work again. . . .*

Cole could see it now . . . and he was just starting to understand what it meant.

He knew what he had to do and where he had
to go.

No matter how dangerous.

SIXTEEN

First, Cole decided to try the official route. Before school started, he headed straight to the library. Ms. Larkin looked at him very curiously when he walked up to her desk. Surely, she remembered him as the boy who had screamed as she shivered.

"Can I help you?" she asked hesitantly.

"I'm working on a report about John Heginbotham, who was hanged here," Cole said in a rush. "I was hoping to go into the archives to research it. I think there's something about him there."

"The archives?" Ms. Larkin was genuinely surprised by Cole's request.

"Yeah. The ones in the sub-basement."

Ms. Larkin regained some of her composure and shook her head. "I'm afraid students aren't allowed to go down there. It's very dangerous. Only historians and city officials are allowed into the archives. I'm sorry."

She didn't seem sorry. She seemed nervous.

"I could ask a teacher to go with me," Cole offered.

But he'd already lost Ms. Larkin, he could tell. She was moving on to other work.

"No," she said, turning to stamp out some books. "Students can't go down there. End of discussion."

The hanged man was waiting for Cole as he left the library. It was as if he already knew what Cole was just figuring out — it was time for Plan B.

Cole had to sneak down to the archives himself.

This was going to be dangerous. If he was caught, he'd probably be kicked out of school for sure. His mother would be disappointed in him for the rest of his life. Nobody would understand.

But there was no other way. Cole knew he had to find the truth. If he didn't, Heginbotham would continue to rampage — and next time, someone might get hurt.

The only way to make him go away was to go underground.

He stopped at his locker before first period, only to find it covered again with paint:

SCREAM FOR US, FREAK BOY!

A surge of anger rushed through Cole; he pounded the locker so hard that he left a dent (and banged up his hand). For a second, he wondered why he was fighting so hard to stay in this school. Would another school be any different, or would something like this happen wherever he went? There were bullies everywhere . . . and dead people everywhere, too.

He endured the taunts in gym class. Mr. Peake was the worst of all, heckling him whenever he missed the ball.

"If you put half as much energy into playing as you do into disrupting the class, you'd be hitting that ball over the net," he wheezed.

Cole tried to ignore him. But the act of ignoring him backhanded its way into paying attention.

Riley wasn't defending him, or even talking to him. Once he tried to tell her he was sorry for snapping at her in the hall, but before he could say anything the volleyball team rotated its position so that he wasn't close to her anymore.

Heginbotham shadowed him through all his classes, waiting for him to make his move. Finally, at lunch Cole decided it was time to try. If anyone asked where he was, he knew Jason would cover for him.

He was free to follow the dead man.

The door to the sub-basement was in an obscure part of the school, near the entrance to the cafeteria kitchen. Cole was relieved to find it unlocked. He was less than relieved to see what was on the other side. He flicked a light switch, but it didn't do much good. Before him was a dimly lit stairway. He couldn't see the bottom.

Heginbotham led him forward, the sound of his footsteps now making sense. The hard, cold echo filled the air. Cole followed him through another doorway and down another stairway. They were in the bowels of the building now, deeper down than graves.

Cole remembered the map. This was where the prisoners were kept. This was where they were taken before they died.

Some of them were still here.

Cole could hear their cries from behind dark doors. The dying gasps. The pleas for mercy. The shouts of contempt.

Heginbotham couldn't hear them. The dead can't hear the other dead.

But Cole could hear them all.

The doors began to open. Cole tried to push through, but the corridor was too narrow, the prisoners' gazes too intent.

Many of them had nooses around their necks.

Some of them had been shot through the heart. The wounds now bled freely, a dark red spilling.

They couldn't all be innocent. Some of them might have been. The rest were kept here by a guilt they could never shed.

There was a man in judge's robes wandering down from the opposite direction. He walked as if blind, feeling the walls as he went, running his hands over dead people he couldn't feel. His expression was one of pain and remorse.

Cole searched desperately for the archives. But all he saw were empty rooms filled with empty screams.

Some of them cried for loved ones. Others cried for forgiveness.

John Heginbotham didn't cry. He led Cole forward.

They were getting close now.

SEVENTEEN

The archives were dank and forgotten, a series of shelves erected in an old cell, rows of ledgers leaning haphazardly against one another. The floor was clean, so Cole figured that a janitor came by every now and then to tidy things up. But the books looked untouched, their secrets safe.

The cries of the dead were still loud in Cole's ears. He'd never heard such a cacophony of guilt and grief. In the corner of the archives, a man in old clothes faced the wall, screaming, "Kill me now! Kill me now!" He did not notice the noose around his neck, or how his eyes bulged out of his head. Cole was afraid he would turn, afraid he would ask for something. What could Cole give a man who wanted to be dead, not knowing he had already been killed?

Heginbotham's death march continued. His eyes seemed clearer now, his step less deranged. Like a man walking to his fate.

He stopped at one of the shelves, leaning against the wall. Hesitantly, Cole followed. He knew that his classmates were only a few dozen feet above his head right now, laughing at jokes, eating hot lunches from the cafeteria, getting books from their lockers for the afternoon's classes. He knew he hadn't gone very far, but it was a world away from him now. He'd always lived with part of his life there and part of his life here, in the world of the dead. Nothing living touched him now. He had crossed over completely.

Heginbotham got to his knees, the noose tightening around his neck. He reached for a book he could no longer hold. Cole took it for him. He figured this would be the answer — this book would be the key to the hanged man's salvation. But when Cole looked he saw that it was a compendium of court budgets from 1867 to 1870. Long after Heginbotham's time.

The dead man reached for another book, which Cole took out. Court budgets from 1871 to 1874. This time Cole opened the book and flipped through it, hoping to find some message in the pages. This made Heginbotham release a guttural moan — a painful, frustrated noise. He made a sudden push at

Cole, who dropped the book. This seemed to satisfy Heginbotham. He pointed to three more books. Cole pulled them out and put them aside. He still couldn't understand — how could court budgets help prove Heginbotham's innocence?

As Cole watched, Heginbotham's noose tightened further. He gasped and choked. He pointed to the space once occupied by the books. Cole looked through and all he could see was the wall on the other side.

The wall.

The walls of the other cells were stone. This one had been plastered over to secure the archives.

"Is there something in the wall?" Cole asked.

Heginbotham was arching his back, tangled by the rope. But Cole thought the dead man heard, thought he nodded.

Cole pounded at the plaster. It gave way a little, but not enough. Heginbotham was flailing his arms now, trying to loosen the rope from his throat. Cole picked up one of the old books and smashed its edge into the wall. The plaster gave way, the shallow wall breaking. Cole reached through the shelf and pulled the plaster apart. Heginbotham cried out, but Cole couldn't understand the words — only their urgency. Behind the plaster was a stone wall. Cole reached to it and found a stone that moved. Heginbotham choked behind him as he leaned into the bookshelves and removed the loose stone. At first he didn't see a thing. Heginbotham shuddered violently on the floor. Then Cole saw the envelope, pressed against the second stone layer of the wall. He reached out and pulled it from where it had sat for almost two hundred years.

Silence.

Cole crawled out from the plaster, books, and stone.

Heginbotham was gone.

The letter was in Cole's hand.

Shakily, he opened it up.

He couldn't believe what he saw.

EIGHTEEN

Cole pressed his ear against the sub-basement door, trying to figure out if there was anyone on the other side. He knew he looked like a wreck; he'd tried to wipe off all the plaster and dust, but some of it clung to him like the memory of screams. Getting here without being seen was only half the risk; now he had to get out okay. He heard a few people pass . . . then nothing. He figured he was as safe as he'd ever be. He opened the door and casually stepped out.

Dennis was waiting for him.

"You think you're so smart, but Dennis is smarter," the bully said, tugging at his overalls. "You're going to go down, boy. Trouble can't even begin to describe the situation you're in."

Cole wondered if Dennis had always been like

this. He wondered if he had always gotten such pleasure out of other people's pain.

Suddenly, Cole was sick of it. He had been holding back. He had let his frustration grow. Dennis wasn't the only bully, but he was the only one Cole could take on. Cole knew that standing up for himself was sometimes dangerous; sometimes being aggressive only made things worse. But he couldn't take this anymore.

"You're not going to do anything to me," Cole said quietly.

"Is that right?" Dennis said tauntingly. "And what's going to stop me?"

"I think you know," Cole said.

"Do I?" Dennis was turning sarcastic. "What could it be? Are you a master at karate? Are you going to tattle on me to the principal? Are you going to have your mommy beat me up? Is that it, you freak?"

"No."

"What is it then? What do you know that I don't know?"

Cole looked him right in the eye. He knew he had to look him right in the eye.

"You're dead, Dennis," he said.

"No, *you're* dead," Dennis snarled. He swung his right fist to hit Cole.

It wouldn't land.

"What?" Dennis cried, staring at his hand. "How did you do that?"

"I didn't do it, Dennis. It's you."

"I'm going to kill you for this."

A few other people had filtered into the hall now, cafeteria workers taking a break from the lunch shift.

"Scream, Dennis," Cole said calmly. "Scream as loud as you can. They won't hear you."

"Shut up," Dennis said. Then he started to yell. "Shut up! SHUT UP!" Louder and louder.

The cafeteria workers didn't turn.

Dennis looked shocked. He turned and ran into the cafeteria with Cole at his heels.

"HEY EVERYBODY!" he shouted.

Nobody heard him.

He climbed on top of one of the tables and shouted again.

"LOOK AT ME! SOMEBODY . . . LOOK AT ME!"

Nobody looked at him . . . except Cole.

"WHAT'S GOING ON?" he cried out. Then he quieted down. "What's going on?"

Cole knew that some of the kids in the cafeteria were looking at him. He knew he couldn't start a conversation with someone who wasn't really there. But Dennis wouldn't let him go.

"Tell me," he implored, stepping off the table. "Tell me what's happening!"

"You know," Cole whispered. "Think about it."

"I'm not dead."

Then it hit. That moment. Cole had seen it before. The shock. The truth. All of the denial peeled away, leaving a raw expression of pure terror and sadness.

"No," Dennis whimpered, suddenly seeming younger, all his toughness drained. He crumpled to the floor, where students walked over him, returning their lunch trays. "I want my mother," he said, turning to Cole. "Please . . . I want my mother . . . her name's Andrea Holden."

"Where does she live?" Cole asked quietly.

"She moved," Dennis replied . . . and then he was lost to tears.

Cole tried to convince him to get up again, but he just stayed there on the floor of the cafeteria, crying as the world went on without him.

NINETEEN

Cole called Detective Brown from the school pay phone and told him about Dennis; Brown said that he'd try to trace the mother, but couldn't promise any results.

It took all Cole's self-control not to skip out on the second half of school. He figured he had taken enough risks for today — leaving early would be pressing his luck. Plus, Heginbotham had waited a long time to have his envelope delivered; an extra three hours wouldn't hurt.

As soon as last period was over, Cole headed to Professor Rohlfing's house. Much to his surprise, the door was answered on the first ring.

"I had a feeling it would be you," the professor said.

Immediately, Cole could sense there was something different. There was a lightness in Rohlfing's tone . . . and in the house, too.

Something had happened.

They sat down again in the parlor. Cole strained to hear the sound of the rocking chair . . . but he couldn't.

"Do you have further questions?" the professor asked. "I have to admit, I'm amazed that you've been given such a thorough assignment at your age."

"It's not that," Cole said. He'd rehearsed this part a lot on his way over. "There's something I have to show you. I found it in the archives."

Professor Rohlfing raised an eyebrow at that. "You were in the archives?"

"Yes. And I found something. I don't know if you know this, but the room that the archives are in used to be John Heginbotham's cell."

"I didn't know that."

"It's in the plans, in the library. Anyway, he left this there. I found it."

Cole took the envelope out of his backpack and handed it to Rohlfing.

"Is this a joke?" Rohlfing asked. But the age of the paper made him take it very seriously. Gently, he pulled the letter from the envelope. When he started reading, he gasped.

In these, the last hours of my life, I wish to ask forgiveness for all that I have done. A burdened man, I have tried to get away with what I have done. That has not worked, perhaps because of a greater Justice that I must answer to. Please do not think me an evil man. I did not set out to betray my friends and my country. I started as a weak man and became even weaker over times. I gambled, and soon owed not only all of my own money but my family's money as well. I could not let that stand. I needed money. I stole secrets and sold them. I have lied to myself and made myself believe in my innocence. But now the voices of dead soldiers and the smell of our burning capitol are too much for me to bear. Forgive me when I am gone. Forgive me for harm I have done. Know that I have been punished and will be eternally guilty. God save me.

JH

"Do you know what this is?" Rohlfing asked.

Cole nodded.

Rohlfing read to the end, then said, "It's his confession."

He wasn't innocent after all. He was guilty. And the reason he was still around was because nobody had ever heard his confession. He needed his guilt to be acknowledged.

Rohlfing was astonished. "This changes everything!" he proclaimed. Then he called upstairs. "Donna, come here! You're not going to believe this."

The professor's wife came down the stairs, asking, "What is it?" Cole recognized her as the woman he'd seen through the window on his first visit here. Only now she looked much less sad.

"It's not your fault," the daughter must have whispered. "You need to know that and believe that."

"Tell me again how you found this," Professor Rohlfing asked. So Cole told him a variation of the truth; he left out the part about Heginbotham being there, of course, and made it sound like he'd figured out the hiding place from the library maps.

"I can't believe I didn't think of that!" Rohlfing exclaimed.

"Maybe it takes a young mind, David," his wife comforted him, winking at Cole.

"And you had permission to go to the archives?" the professor asked Cole.

Cole was afraid he would ask that.

"Not really," he mumbled.

"Well, nobody has to know that," Rohlfing said. "With your permission, I'd like to head over there today and 'find' this document myself. Then we can run the tests to make sure it's legitimate, and if it is, I'll have a whole new spin for my next article. I might even write a book!"

It was clear that Rohlfing was going to be working again . . . and it seemed like his wife was happy about that, too.

Cole hoped that their daughter knew this, wherever she was now. He hoped she was proud.

As he walked back home from the Rohlfings' house, Cole thought about how strange it was that so many people could be so randomly connected to one another. The truth about a man who was hanged was somehow connected to a teenage girl who was killed in a car crash two hundred years later. The future of a dead boy looking for his mother was connected to a police detective whose brother disappeared because he could see dead people. And they were all connected to Cole. In some mysterious way, he bound them all together.

But his closest tie was still waiting for him at home, ready with a weary smile when he stepped through the door. This was the tie that kept him connected to this world, to this life. This was the tie that saved him time and again.

"How was your day?" his mother asked him as he took off his coat. Such a simple question, and it seemed so enormous. How was his day? How could he even begin to describe his day?

So instead of giving an answer, he laughed. And inside that laugh, there was fear and relief. Lynn Sear took one look at her soon and understood this. She reached over and pulled Cole close to her. She knew the fine line between a laugh and a sob. She knew that both were necessary in order to make it through life.

Over dinner, he told her about the hanged man and Professor Rohlfing's daughter. Then he told her about Dennis. As he told her, he felt better, because telling someone else about it all made it more real . . . almost normal. His mom wasn't happy about what he was saying — she would never be happy that her son saw dead people — but she wasn't doubting him, either. She knew she wasn't expected to give him answers. All she had to do was listen.

Then it was Cole's turn to listen, as his mom told him about looking for jobs and trying to plan out what would come next.

"I'll be able to work at Moira's shop for a while, so

we're not going to starve. But I want to take a little time to figure out where I'm going from here. I was so caught up in working at that awful place that I never really thought about what I wanted to do. So maybe this whole thing was a blessing. Maybe I'll be able to find out what I'm meant to do. You'll have to bear with me, okay?"

"I want you to be happy, Mom," Cole said.

"Thank you, Cole."

They had double dessert that night. And maybe it was because of the chocolate overload, or maybe it was because it was unseasonably warm in Philadelphia, but that night Cole slept soundly. Instead of nightmares, he had dreams of amusement park rides and volleyball championships.

The dead kept their distance. He didn't even know they were there.

TWENTY

Lynn Sear was waiting for Cole outside school the next day. At first he thought she was picking him up on the way home from an errand. Then he saw the piece of paper in her hand.

"Nineteen Robbins Lane, Lambertville, New Jersey," she said when Cole got to the car. "Detective Brown called me a few minutes ago. That's where Andrea Holden lives. Her son, Dennis, died twenty-one years ago. He was a very sick child — leukemia. He went to this school."

Cole nodded.

"Is he here now?" Lynn asked.

"I've got to go get him."

* * *

On the way to the cafeteria, Cole saw Riley.

"Can I talk to you for a second?" he asked.

She nodded and said, "Go ahead."

He let the words out in a rush. "I'm sorry I snapped at you in the halls the other day. There was just too much going on, and everybody was watching me. I know you were helping and I wanted to say thank-you for that."

"You're welcome."

"Really?"

Riley smiled. "Yeah. We strange kids have to stick together, don't we?"

Cole had to agree.

The cafeteria was empty, the tables cleared for wrestling practice. Dennis was still curled up in the same spot, rocking convulsively.

"Dennis," Cole said, leaning over so he could hear. "I think we've found your mom. You need to come with me."

Dennis looked at him, bewildered. Then he stood . . . and followed.

Lynn kept looking in the rearview mirror at the back seat, even though she couldn't see the boy sitting there.

Neither she nor Cole said a word. There didn't

seem anything right to say. Instead they drove in silence — the quiet, breathing silence of the living.

It was nearing dusk when they arrived. They'd gotten a little lost getting off of the highway. But now the house numbers were counting down to their destination — 51 ROBBINS LANE . . . 43 . . . 29 . . .

19.

There was a woman in the front garden, planting perennials. The minute Lynn saw her, she began to cry. Cole felt choked up, too. But none of their reactions could match Dennis's.

He knew she was there before he saw her. He'd been lying back with his eyes closed the whole ride. Now he was up at the window, pressing against the glass.

"Mom!" he cried.

He was out of the car. He was running toward her.

As Cole watched Dennis stumble across the front yard, Lynn watched Dennis's mother. She had been planting happily, pleasantly occupied. Now she put down her spade and shivered. She looked around for the wind. She stood up.

She knows, Lynn thought. *A mother must know.*

Dennis stopped in front of her. He didn't even

notice that she wasn't looking directly at him. All he needed to know was that she was there.

Cole saw Dennis embrace his mother, wrapping her in his arms, drawing her as close as he could. Lynn saw Dennis's mother open her arms and hold the empty space, moving her hands to hold tight.

She knows . . .

Cole closed his eyes, and when he opened them, Dennis was gone. His mother stood alone in her garden, standing in a wind that had just started to blow.

Lynn fought the urge to go out to the mother, to let her know what had happened. Then she realized she didn't really have to explain. The moment — the sensation — would explain itself.

Lynn reached over for Cole's hand and squeezed it tight. He squeezed back.

We're here. We're together.

No matter what.

As Lynn pulled the car away, Cole stole one last look back at Dennis's mother. Imagining her grief, he felt such sadness and frustration and pain. Imagining the joy she might feel from this one moment, he felt in some small way like he'd helped. He felt weakness and strength, tumult and peace.

Such was the power of his sixth sense.